Don't Blame Me

Don't Blame Me

Acknowledgments

This book is a bit different as it is my very first full length novel. This was a journey as it was a different process and required so much extra research and patience.

. First, I want to thank A.E. Snow my fabulous editor and an amazing woman, author and friend. Thank you for always working with me and helping me get my stuff terrible to readable. You are simply the best with working with me and my schedule and all the things life throws at me.

Next, I wanted to thank Marina for supporting my first full length project. You have been telling me to do this since 2014 and I thank you for your continued support.

Cindy, thank you or giving me Taylor Swift's album Reputation. I heard the song Don't Blame Me, and the lyrics spoke to me as I wrote Adrian.

Day, thank you for all the questions you answered about college football because man oh man I had no idea. And allowing me to bounce the ideas off of you with football positions and stats. (Smile).

B.P, thanks for the insight on magazines. I couldn't have done this without you.

M.L thanks for going over the Hawaiian phrases for me. Brittany (my soul sister) and Rye thanks for listening to me complain, doubt myself and all the other things we discussed via Instagram. Thanks for your feedback and your support.

You guys made this so much more enjoyable. I love you two.

Mom, thank you for your continued support eve when I doubt myself.

To my Cubs, my babies, thank you for choosing me to be your mom. I love you all.

Last, but not least. Thank you readers for continuing my journey with me and your continued support. I couldn't do this without you.

Author's Note:

While there is football in this book, it isn't the sole basis of the book. The main focus is the romance. The college, the college football team, the school's location and other stuff associated with the football aspects are fiction.

If any of the football aspects seems to resemble something else or someone else it is purely coincidental.

I do hope you enjoy.

Xoxo

Kay

Chapter One

Adrian

(2016)

It was going to be a long day. I was opening a new hotel. A new hotel in New York City. I sighed in relief as I drank the dark coffee in my thermal cup. I was running on little sleep and one there was a lot of work to do. Today was going to be one of those days.

My cell rang, interrupting my morning thoughts, and I answered it.

"Good morning. This is Adrian speaking."

"Good morning Mr. Robinson. This is Dana Hopkins from Dana Magazine. We've decided to do something a little different this time. Something, a bit more fun for the magazine. Our sister magazine Inner Circle did the Top 15 most eligible bachelors in the world. You were one of the top

15. We decided to piggyback off of it, and do a spread on you since you're opening the new hotel in NYC."

"Oh wow. Really? That's an honor. Thank you."

"No, thank you for answering so quickly. One of our writers here will be doing a profile piece about you. I will send the email to you once we end this call."

"Okay. Great. Thanks for this. I've never been an eligible bachelor before," I said with a laugh.

She laughed. "Well, we have never done this before. But, since we are based in New York, we thought we would do a whole work-up profile piece for you. The hotel opening will be like the bonus."

"Sounds great. I will look at my schedule and have my assistant get the details to you."

"Perfect Mr. Robinson. Talk to you soon."

"Great. Have a good one," I replied before ending the call.

I heard the ping go off on my phone, and opened the new message from Dana Magazine. My eyes skimmed through the email until I saw a familiar name on the screen.

Once I realized who it was, I almost knocked over my coffee. This kind of reaction hadn't happened to me in years. Something that only happened with her. Only her. And after all this time, even just seeing her name, she still did something to me.

The email stated that Leah Hunter will be writing a profile/interview article that showcased me not only opening my hotel in New York, but also mentioning that I was one of the world's most eligible bachelors. I would be seeing Leah again after all this time. Leah was the girl I lost all those years ago. She had so many plans when we went to school together, and here she was doing all the things she said she would and more. It was one of the things that I loved about her. I wondered if she was still the same person she was back then.

What were the odds that a woman that I used to be in a relationship with, was writing a whole article about me being one of the most eligible bachelors? It had to be fate. I was destined to see her again.

Part of me wondered if she still felt angry about how things ended between the two of us. Sure, I knew I was the one who royally fucked up. But a guy could still hope, right?

After typing a quick response to the email to confirm that the message was received. I put my phone in my pocket and made my way to my office. I used to be the guy that everyone wanted to be. I had all the girls. Lots of talent and good looks. As cocky as it sounded, I had it all. But years after all of that, I realized those things really didn't interest me anymore. Here I was now, one of the most eligible bachelors, and yet I didn't really do the things that bachelors technically did

My dad owned a bunch of hotels. He started his first when I was a freshman in high school. After college, I decided to join the family business, and I was good at it. Really good at it. Not too long after that, I opened two hotels. And now I was opening up one in Leah's hometown of New York City.

I had come across tons of women, and, my secretary Lydia told me that many of the women guests checked in because I was good looking. I had hoped it was because I made sure to give a wonderful experience at my hotels. However, she didn't believe it and felt the commercials I did, and the ads that I was in all contributed to why women came to my hotels in droves. Many repeat guests and good reviews. I made sure exceptional service was given to every single guest.

I admit I didn't always want this for my life. I had big dreams of getting into the NFL and showing the world how dominant I could be on the field. I was a damn good at it too. Playing the outside linebacker position had opened doors for me. Those doors closed after I got my injury. Life certainly had a way of changing things for you and forcing you to work with what was left. While I wasn't too bad with my grades, football was my life. But my dad only ever saw this vision that he had for me. And my mother wanted to brag about her son, the football star. Both pulled me in two different directions. Neither really listened to what I wanted.

"Morning, boss!" she said, her voice chipper, as I walked towards her desk.

"Morning, Lydia. I got a call about being voted as one of the most eligible bachelors in the US. Crazy, right?"

"No. It isn't. I think that sounds pretty cool."

I laughed. I laughed. "I need you to look at my schedule and email Dana magazine. I need to confirm dates for the interview they want for the magazine."

"Of course. Anything else?"

But I didn't respond. My mind was still stuck on Leah writing the article.

"You okay?"

"Yeah, I'm fine. It's nothing."

And maybe that would've been true if it was something else on my mind. Anyone else. But it wasn't that. And she wasn't just anyone. She was Leah. My beautiful hell raiser.

Lydia raised her brow but said nothing more about it. And for once I was glad. I was glad that she didn't pry. No one knew about Leah. No one in my present life did. The only people who knew about her were my parents. And of course Tommy. My parents for some unknown reason didn't particularly like Leah. My mom had made that very clear. I suspected as I got older it was because I was her only child. Her only son. Now, Leah was like a ghost of my past. A ghost I thought I had let go, but it seemed that maybe I was wrong. Leah was very much still in my system. Very much so.

I pulled open the desk drawer and pulled out a picture frame. I stood it up on the desk. It was one of those wooden plain black frames, with the one picture that I still had left from my days of college. Well, the one picture that I had that included Leah. It was a night after my team had won one of the most important games of the seasons. We had decided to go out and celebrate with some of the other people on the team, and this picture was snapped. Neither one of us was looking at the camera. She looked at me. I looked at her. Smiles on our faces. Lost in each other. We were genuinely happy and the picture had captured it. Of course, this was before things went to shit with us. And even to this day, I regretted how it played out in the end. I knew my indifference and attitude was the reason we were apart in the first place. I couldn't blame her though. I was a major egotistical asshole back then.

You know what Adrian? I regret this. I regret being with you. You're not worth this. I knew this all along and I told myself I was making too much of it. I wished I would've listened. But it doesn't matter now. You're not worth this kind of pain. And eventually, it won't bother me anymore. You will have to live with the fact that you messed up something good. I hope this bothers you every single day for the rest of your fucking life.

I remembered the angry tears that ran down her face, her shoulders heaving. But I didn't comfort her. The damage was already done and my ego let her walk away.

Sighing, I took the frame and placed it back and closed the drawer. I opened my laptop and typed in her name. A picture of her from an event last year popped up. I clicked on it.

God damn, she was still beautiful. Still my Leah.

All of her accolades and publications had come up. While she mostly focused on women's issues, and issues that women of color face, she would occasionally do what was considered a soft piece on various subjects. Even though I would see her soon, a small part of me couldn't wait to hear her voice again. Or look into her big russet colored eyes. I wanted to touch her brown skin. A bigger part of me hoped that I could kiss those full lips of hers one more time.

I grunted and clicked off the links, it was no point in going down memory lane. That part of my life was over. Mostly because I fucked up back then, but it didn't mean that I didn't miss her. If she was still the woman she was when we were in college, then I know she would have no parts of it. And I couldn't blame her.

After looking over the numbers on the spreadsheet, I looked at the time. I had a meeting to go to soon. The grand opening for the new hotel was coming up, and knowing my father, he would be up my ass about making sure everything went well without a hitch. He was like that for most things, but when it came to the hotels, he was a whole different beast.

After a few emails and conference calls, I watched as the doors to my office opened and my father walked in. As usual, he walked in without knocking. He strolled in like he owned the place. Yeah, we were in a business together, but this was my office. He always wore expensive suits and had this aura about him that let everyone else know he was a man of importance and money. One of the things that attracted my mother to him at first.

"Nice to see you Dad," I said sarcastically, already sensing that there was going to be a long-winded conversation about what he thought would be best.

"Did you set up the flights to California? You have to be there in two days," he said ignoring my statement.

"Yes. You know Lydia does the flights and whatnot. That is what she is paid for."

Of course, I saw Lydia as a good friend, but no need to let my dad know that or he would want to fire her right away.

"And the conference calls?"

"All handled."

"You know I heard from your assistant that you were picked for one of the most eligible bachelors. She couldn't stop gushing about it. I don't know why she's under the impression that we were friends. I didn't know you were into that kind of thing."

"Lydia is a great assistant. I'm not. At least not intentionally. You were the one who wanted me to be in magazines and television ads. Someone did their homework on me. And I am one of many. It isn't a big deal," I said my tone even. My dad always knew how to push my buttons. It was one of the reasons our relationship was the way it was.

"By now you should know what's more important."

I knew what he meant without him having to say anything else. House of Robinson, are top of the line hotels with no room for anything, but perfection. To my dad, nothing else came before business or his hotels. They were his babies. I was glad that the one in NYC would be the one that I would have the most control over. It was a shame that I was using this to get away from my parents, but sometimes they were much too overbearing. Much too pushy and much too worried about what I did in my life. It was frustrating. Even as a grown man they were always interjecting themselves into what I did with my life. It was fucking annoying. I loved them, but their constant over the top behavior took a toll on me

"I know Dad. Are there any other words of wisdom that you want to share with me?" I asked sarcastically.

I could see his brow furrow quickly, before the cool and collected expression he usually wore replaced it.

"Call your mother. She has been harassing me because she thinks you're avoiding her." He gave a wave of his hand as if the conversation as dismissed. I watched him walk back out of the room sucking all of the good energy I had in it.

I appreciated him as my father, and all that he taught me to be able to run a hotel successfully, but sometimes he was just too much. Cynical and a perfectionist. While he was fine with me playing football in college, he didn't want a son in the NFL. I was supposed to follow his lead and be in the hotel business. Sometimes it seemed he was glad that I got injured. He never cared too much about my feelings about football.

Even though Dana Magazine already confirmed the details about the interview, and when I would need to come in,

I was impatient. A part of me wasn't sure I could wait that long to talk to Leah. I debated if I should call her or send her an email. After realizing I wasn't quite ready to talk to her over the phone, I opened up my email tab and clicked on a new message. I typed in the address I got from Lydia. I wrote the message several times not wanting to sound too desperate. After erasing for the 6th time, I decided to keep it short and friendly.

Good Morning, Leah

Good Morning, Leah

I hope all is well. You're probably already aware we are scheduled to do an interview this upcoming month, but I thought I'd send you an email. We haven't seen each other in years, and I thought it would be nice to catch up over drinks before then. I'm sure you're busy, but please call me at your earliest convenience. Any time.

Best,

A

I added my phone number at the end of it and after a few moments of hesitation, I clicked the sent button.

Immediately I regretted it, but I had to talk to her eventually.

One, I would be in NYC for an extended period of time. Two,

she would be interviewing me. And three, I missed the hell out

of her. Missed her far more than I was willing to admit before.

So, why not get rid of the awkwardness beforehand.

"Alright, now to get ready for California," I said to no

one in particular as I closed my laptop.

Chapter Two

Leah

(2016)

I rolled my eyes hard as I read the email that I was sent. What kind of shit was this? I was still seething at the fact that Dana thought this was a good thing for me. So what if we went to school together? Big freaking deal. I was the absolute worst person to do this for the magazine. Adrian Kai Mahina Robinson was an asshole. The worse kind at that. The heartbreaking kind.

Okay, so maybe I didn't always feel that way. At one point I even loved him. Loved him more than I ever loved anyone. I think there was a small part of me that maybe even still loved him. But time had a habit of changing things, and now he was attached to bad memories from my past. He was the past that I kept locked away and most of the time ignored when I thought about my time at Ocean View. Ocean View University was a good school and I had a good time the two years that I attended. And then everything went to hell. I transferred after my second year and moved back to NY to finish school. Adrian was a piece of fucking work. And now, of course, my boss thought it would be nice for me to interview him because I know him. I knew him. Past tense. Didn't know shit about him now. Nor did I want to.

Dana had no idea that we were much more than old school chums. In college, Adrian was everything to me. My be all and end all. There was a point where we were so into each other nothing else mattered. I would even go as far to say there was a slight obsession on my part. Not obsession like crazy. An obsession like one an addict has with a drug, and I could have him all the time, any time. I didn't think rationally around him. He consumed me or rather I let him. He burned my soul and filled too much of it. Way too much. But, that was then, and this is now. I wouldn't be going down that road again.

Besides, after everything that happened, I wasn't sure I could face him. Because when it all mattered, he was a coward and it still bothered me, even after all this time.

"Dana, do I really have to do this article? I mean I'm sure Cindy could write this, she likes this kind of stuff. I am not even into bachelors and their eligibility. I couldn't care less," I said with an attitude. Inside I was livid and fuming. But Dana was always looking out for me, so I couldn't be too mad. But, bachelors? Adrian? Of course, everyone had their preferences on what I wanted to read. I just wished I wasn't a part of it.

"I know you don't normally do these kinds of pieces for the magazine, but it would be nice if you do something outside the box for you. You come across as tough as nails and well you know..." she said.

"Bitchy?"

"No! I don't think anything about you is bitchy at all. I love your work ethic. Though sometimes you need to loosen up. But definitely not bitchy. Not bitchy at all. I will say this though, you need to soften up just a little, that's all."

I rolled my eyes. It was something I did so often that I was sure it somehow encoded into my DNA.

"Are you rolling your eyes at me?" Dana asked me half seriously.

Yes, she was my boss. But she was also my friend and I needed her to understand just how annoyed all of this was making me.

"Sorry Dana I'm over the moon about this," I said sarcastically.

"Mhmmm. Well, it is not like you have to personally contact him. I set all of that up already. I know he will be flying into the city soon for his opening. I will like you to interview him and have all the things you need before the grand opening of the hotel. I want it to be in unison in a way. This will also be great exposure for the magazine. And for you. You act like he's an asshole or something. I've heard nothing but good things about him."

"That's convenient," I mumbled.

"Did you know him personally? I know you two shared the same school, but that's it."

"You could say that."

Dee raised her eyebrow and then a sly smile came over her face.

"Oh, you guys had a thing in college, huh? How was he?" she said talking more like my friend than my boss.

"Key word there is college. We were a thing and college and now we aren't. We shouldn't have been a thing back then if you asked me, but what do I know. I am just a woman who needs to loosen up and apparently talk to ex-boyfriends to do so," I said quickly still heated about all of this. Still hoping that maybe, just maybe she would change her mind about me doing this in the first place.

"That bad, huh? Well, look at it like this, how long has it been ten years?"

"Twelve."

"Okay, twelve years. I am sure he is different from the college football star he was in college. Look at it this way, it's a job and nothing else. Once you're finished, you can go on about your life and keep writing the fabulous articles that you write. If it'll make you feel any better you can even forget that he exists once you're done."

"I guess. You're so lucky that I love you as both my boss and my friend. Because if I didn't…"

"Uh huh. I love you too. You got work to do missy."

Dana walked out of my office and I sat back in my leather chair, closed my eyes and sighed heavily. This shouldn't have been this hard. Dana was right, this was nothing but a job. I have done way more complicated articles than this. There was the one I did on breast cancer and on depression. The lists was extensive. It was hard being a black woman in this writing gig, so I worked my ass off. But even so, for some reason, this one bothered me the most. I typed in his name and looked up what he had been up to. Adrian had taken the hotel world by storm. I knew he was smart. But it was different than me saying so when we were in college. It seemed he had a real knack for hotels.

I couldn't help but wonder if any part of the person he was in college was still there. Was he still a jerk with a huge personality that almost made it too hard to breathe? Or worse for me was he still the person that consumed almost all of me and almost burned me to cinders. I couldn't have that happen again. I had to make sure that we kept it professional. Nothing outside of getting what I needed to write the best damn article about him and then quickly move back on with the life I had for the last twelve years. Easy peasy. Right?

Checking my email, I saw his name in my mailbox. Speak of the devil. I opened the email he had sent. He sounded too friendly for me, and it annoyed the fuck out of me. If my gut was right, this was his way of taking charge of this situation. He never did like to wait on things, and I could see by this email, he wanted to chat before I scheduled a meeting. After a few moments, I picked up my office phone and dialed the number that he had left at the bottom of the email.

After two rings, I heard some scuffles and then a deep voice came onto the phone. It was like music to my ears and I cringed. How was it possible for his voice to get any deeper than it was in college? And worse, why did it still get a reaction out of me? I felt that all the way down to my core and I hated it. I hated him at that moment.

"Hello?" he asked.

"Hello. It's Leah Hunter," I said as if he didn't know who I was.

"Hey, Leah. How are you?"

"I'm good. You?"

"Fine. Busy with all the things that are going on with this new hotel, but fine. I'm surprised you called."

I thought about that. I didn't know how surprised he could possibly be when we both knew this interview had to take place, but I decided instead to be nice and save my usual sarcastic response.

"I thought it would be easier to talk via the phone rather than email. I don't know if there's a reason to meet up beforehand though. I'm sure you're a busy man."

"I'll be there at the end of the week. How's Friday? We can do a late lunch around two in the afternoon?" he said, completely ignoring what I said.

"Did you hear what I said?"

"I did. But it would be nice to see you before we get down to business."

I groaned inwardly, remembering what Dana had said. It was a job. And I knew she would want me to be nice.

"Fine. What do you suggest?"

"How about lunch on Friday afternoon? We can eat and chat a little. I'm always doing business meetings, so I rather not jump right into business with you since we were friends at one point."

Friends? Sure, if that's what he wanted to call it.

I glanced at my calendar and realized that I did have some free time during the afternoon on Friday.

"Okay. Lunch on Friday. Do you have a place in mind?"

"Yeah. There is this restaurant that is near the location of the hotel, we can meet there and grab a bite to eat, and then you can tell me what you need from me for this article," he said.

I listened to the way he took charge, and a part of me was impressed. He had certainly grown up. He sounded confident and self-assured. I liked it. Different from the cocky jock he was back then. Well, this may be easier than I thought it would be.

"That works. What's the address?"

He gave me the address and I wrote it down on my notepad with the date and time. I had to remember to add this into my phone's schedule. My phone was my life. Everything was on it. All of my life was on it.

"Okay, Adrian. I will see you then."

"It was nice talking to you again Leah."

"Uh huh. Ok. Talk to you soon," I said, hanging up the phone quickly. I didn't like that he was trying to have a different conversation. I was doing my job. Nothing more. Nothing less. He would just have to accept that I wasn't the girl I was in college. I had other things that I cared about, and he was no longer one of them.

I sent a quick email to Dee to let her know that the meeting was scheduled. Realizing that it was past the time I should eat something, I went into my bag and pulled out an apple. I could always eat later. I had another article to finish, and I didn't want to miss my deadline.

On Friday afternoon I walked up to the address that Adrian had given me. It was a fancy looking place. I walked until I found the maître d', an extremely pale woman with her hair in a tight bun.

"Good afternoon," she said once she saw me.

"Good afternoon, I am here to see Adrian Robinson for a two o'clock reservation."

"Sure, he is waiting for you at the table. Right this way," she said.

I nodded and followed her passed many tables until we were in a more private section of the restaurant. I could see him as I got closer and my heart skipped a beat. Damn it. Damn him to hell. Why did he still have this effect on me after all this time?

As I reached the table where he sat, I could see his brown eyes light up and he looked me up and down appreciatively. He stood up as we walked to the table. Now I was questioning if the white blouse I wore was much too tight for this lunch. I didn't need him studying me. I needed to get this lunch over with as quickly as possible.

"Here you go, ma'am," the maître d' said.

"Thank you," I replied.

"Thank you, Helena," Adrian said and his voice was even deeper than it was on the phone.

He came to me a wide smile on his face, and he pulled me in for a hug. I froze as his big arms wrapped around me. They were more muscular now and still huge. He was still massive at his 6'3" height and immediately I felt overwhelmed. He was always overwhelming. Always too big for any room. It was still the same. He was overpowering. I felt myself tremble a little, and I moved out of his grip.

"Hey," I said weakly.

"Hey, Leah. You look great. Really great. It's been forever," he said.

His smile was genuine. I studied him. His jaw more chiseled. Stronger. The suit that he wore fit him well, I might add. And his muscles had grown since college. His dark hair was much longer now. He wore it in a ponytail and my knees started to feel weak. I'd thought that maybe the memories will hold their place in my heart as they have always done before, but I had no such luck. They came back with such a force, that I grabbed the back of the chair to steady myself. I could still feel his lips on my skin. His big hands touching me gently, always wanting more even when I wanted to pull away. I licked my lips and backed away slightly.

"Let me get that for you," he said, moving towards me to pull the chair out for me to sit.

"Thank you," I said softly, watching as he sat down across from me.

"How have you been?" he asked.

"Working mostly. I don't have too much of a life outside of that. Working and living as much as I can with the little time I do have," I replied. "You?"

"Same. Running a hotel is a lot of work. And with overbearing parents, well you know."

I nodded. I did know. His parents and mine were alike in that way.

"When I saw that I was chosen as one of the most eligible bachelors, I admit I was a bit surprised. I didn't know they still did those kinds of things. But, then I got the initial call from your boss that you would do a separate piece to tie in with the hotel that I'm opening. Once I saw that you would be interviewing me, I was shocked, in a good way. Who knew the universe would throw us back together."

"My boss thought it would be nice since we went to the same school."

"I figured it had to be something like that. Does she know about our past?"?

"No. Well, she didn't at first. I just told her that once upon a time we were a thing, and that is it. I didn't want to bore her with all the details. Besides, it wasn't necessary," I said, moving my hair out of my face.

I tried looking at everything but him. It wasn't that I was trying to be rude, but he always had a way that he looked at me, and he was doing it now. He looked through my soul. I hated that he knew how to do that. He always took up way too much space in my head and heart. He was overbearing, and he had no idea that he did that to me.

"I thought we could eat first, and then we can talk and catch up."

I nodded. "Okay."

The waiter came over to us.

"Would you like something to drink?" he asked.

"How about your finest bottle of wine," Adrian responded. I nodded. Wine was needed.

"And would you like an appetizer, sir?"

"Are you ready to order?" Adrian asked me.

"Uh, hold on." I quickly scanned the menu. "Can I get the spinach ravioli?" I asked.

"And you, sir?"

"You can get me the same," Adrian replied looking at me.

Once the waiter left, I could feel Adrian staring at me. I wondered what he was thinking. What did he want to say to me? I really just wanted to get this article over with. Seeing him stirred up old feelings and old wounds. Way too many things I didn't want to relive again, and then there was something that was still there lying underneath all these things I've been feeling.

"So, it's been years. Besides working, what have you been doing with yourself?" he asked me.

I paused, trying to think how to answer that question without sounding like the biggest bore in all of history.

"Uh, that's just it for the most part. As I told you earlier, I really don't do much else. You?"

"Mostly working with my father. Traveling a bit. This hotel in New York is my baby. You have no idea how happy I am that it is. Gives me a chance to spread my wings and not be under my dad's shadow. It's like ever since I decided to do this with him, I'm living in his shadow and the shadow of my past with football."

"Oh. I knew your father had ties to this. I'm sure he's happier that you are doing this, rather than playing football," I said bluntly. Quickly, I apologized. "I'm sorry. I didn't mean to sound so much like... well, you know a reporter. I just remember he really wasn't a big fan of you playing football."

"That's fine. I mean it is what it is now. I can't change what happened with me and my dad. Now, we work together as best as we can, and that's about it. He's a stubborn man."

"Yeah, I do. You're pretty stubborn yourself."

"Is that so?"

I raised my eyebrow for dramatic effect. "Am I wrong?"

Adrian laughed. "No. You're not. I was stubborn. Still am to an extent. I think I've gotten better with making compromises."

"Well, thank God for small miracles," I said jokingly and we laughed.

I hated to admit that it was nice laughing with him. It almost made me forget all of that other shit that had happened with the two of us. *Almost.*

"You know it would seem you have gotten more beautiful than the last time I saw you. The picture under your articles doesn't do you justice."

"You looked up pictures of me online?"

"No. Well, I didn't until recently. I read some of the articles you wrote after I found out I would be seeing you again. You always were a damn good journalist. I couldn't bring myself to keep up with what you did after we split up though. It was too painful. Sorry!" He shrugged and took a sip from the glass in front of him. It looked like bourbon.

"How are your parents?" he asked.

"Um…hopefully at peace. I lost them both a few years back. My mother went two years after my dad did."

His face softened. "I'm sorry to hear that."

Besides, even though they were pushy sometimes, I do still have good memories of them."

I found myself looking around before looking back at his expression, which seemed sad.

"So, are you happy running a hotel empire," I asked him needing something else to talk about.

"I mean I've grown to love it. I didn't like it too much at first. I did it mostly because I was angry about my football career getting cut short, and partially to get my parents off my back. Now, I like it. I like talking to people. Being an outgoing person has its perks."

I nodded. He did. He could talk someone into many things. It was one of the things I both liked and disliked about him. He always was a bit of a flirt and knew how to say the right things. I was sure he used those same kinds of techniques to run his business.

"I admit that I wasn't really happy that I had to do this. Mostly because I didn't want to see you. I just thought it was opening a can of worms. But at the end of the day, I pride myself in doing my job, so that's what it is."

"And you weren't at all intrigued that somehow I made it onto a list of the most eligible bachelors?"

"No. Not really. Not to say it isn't a good thing. It is. I'm sure there are plenty of women still hoping to find the perfect bachelor, so this is perfect for them. I am all for women doing what makes them happy. But you have always been an attractive guy and able to do what you seriously put your mind to. So, it isn't too much of a surprise that you made the list."

Adrian nodded at me with appreciation. The waiter placed our orders in front of us and filled our wine glasses with the wine that Adrian had picked out. I could feel his eyes on me again, and so I focused on my food instead. We ate in an uncomfortable silence. At least I was uncomfortable. I made a mental note of the things that he had said that I could include in the article. I could feel the heat from his stare and I looked up to see that his eyes were still on me.

"Is there something on my face that you aren't telling me about?"

"No. I would tell you if there was something."

"You have done that before."

He chuckled. "You got me. But, that was different. We are both adults now."

I shook my head in amusement thinking about the many times he joked around and acted like he didn't know why I would be annoyed.

"You ever think about what we had. What we lost?" he asked me.

Blinking a few times in shock, I put my fork down on my plate. I didn't expect this conversation to be brought up so soon. I'd been dancing around this topic all week. We were something, and now we not. The best way to put it.

I thought about what he had said. Of course, I did. Much longer than I wanted to. He had hurt me both intentionally and unintentionally. And unknown to him, I carried that hurt with me for a long time, and when I saw his name again it brought back all of those feelings. The pain. The pushing and pulling. All of it. And the sex. Man the sex. I felt the color rise in my cheeks. I decided to lie instead.

"No. Not really. It doesn't make sense to dwell too much on the past. It does nobody any good to do that sort of thing."

Who was I kidding? I was the queen of that. But there was no sense of pointing that out there because he didn't need to know that. And most importantly, nothing was going to happen between the two of us ever again.

"I do. A lot. More than I rather admit, but it's true. I wish things ended differently."

"I used to think about that too. I mean things ending differently than it did."

And it was true. But I was staying away from the minefield. However, there was a part of me that wouldn't admit that sometimes I did miss him. And I hated myself for it. It made me think about college and the topsy-turvy relationship we had. He was so bad for me, but for some reason, I was addicted to him like a feen to a drug. And as with most drugs, the withdrawals were fucking brutal.

Chapter Three

Adrian

Ocean View University, Florida (2004)

It was twenty minutes after practice and I walked back to my

dorm room, high off the adrenaline. Ever since training camp

all of us made sure to give it our all, even in practice, because

the season started in a week. I was ready for it all. I was

Adrian Kai Mahina Robinson. The best damn linebacker,

Ocean View had ever seen.

As usual, I was looking for something to get into or

someone to get into. It wasn't like I didn't have the girls on

campus eating out of my hand, because I did. But my motto

was to never be with one woman for too long of a time. I was

young and mostly carefree. Girls tended to want to get too

attached and expect a relationship, and I didn't have time for that. I was a football star on campus and I knew I would be one in the NFL one day. I was in my junior year of college and I was a damn good player at all. So, I kept my prospects open all the time. I didn't need to be tied down. I played hard and worked hard. College was supposed to be for those things right? Football and Fun. Fun and football. No in between. What could be better than that?

I made my way across campus to my dorm room. I shared a room with my Tommy. We were both on the team. He was the quarterback and I was a linebacker. Two different parts of the team, but one big machine. He was my best friend and the one who dealt with all my crap mostly.

As I made my way across the field that led to my dorm, I saw a girl walking with a tight skirt on and a shirt that showed all of her cleavage. She had nice big breasts. Being the guy I was, of course, I stared. I turned around to walk backward, watching as the girl waved and I smiled. Maybe I should head in her direction. I stepped once more, and knocked into something, or rather someone.

Turning around, a girl stood there, bending down, as she picked up her books from the floor. I went to help her and she shook her head in a silent no. She stood up, her brown hair blew in her face and over her eyes from the wind. Her brow furrowed with anger.

"You really need to watch where you're going?" she said.

"I'm sorry. I wasn't paying attention," I replied with a shrug.

"Obviously," she said with a slight sniffle.

It was then that I realized that something seemed off. As if she was crying. Usually, I would ignore any girl crying because I didn't like tears. Actually, it was one of the things I tried to steer away from. But as she stood there her eyes watery, I felt uncomfortable.

"Uh, are you okay?" I asked, shifting my feet a little feeling awkward. This wasn't my norm. I usually didn't care about this kind of thing, but her face looked so sad. Sad and pretty at the same time.

She looked up at me then, moving her hair out of her face as if that would help her see me better. Wiping her face, she shook her head no.

"No. But I will be. Thanks for asking," she said and then she continued on her path.

She was pretty. Really pretty. Her brown skin was damn near glowing. It threw me off, but only for a few seconds. I wasn't chasing after any girl. As I watched her fleeting figure, I realized that I really didn't care anymore. I shrugged and kept it moving. Once I reached my dorm room, I crashed on my bed, still elated from my practice. Coach had said that there were many prospects looking at me this year, and I was excited about that. It wasn't like I was one of those guys who had a bad upbringing and was using this to get a new life. Sure, having money that was my own would be great, but my mom was well off, and my dad was rich. Rich enough that I never wanted for anything. We didn't really agree on things, and I really didn't care about it. Nobody or nothing was going to stop me from playing football. I didn't care who it pissed off.

I put the remote on my television on and lowered the volume. Flipping through the channels, I stopped when it reached one of those channels that played music. Not really something I wanted to watch, but it was okay. I was tired anyway. Not even five minutes later I felt my eyes getting heavy.

About three hours later, I woke up and realized that I napped longer than I wanted to. I looked at the clock on my desk and got up. I had tons of homework to do, but right now I had more pressing matters to attend to, like letting off a little bit of steam. I knew who would be willing to have a little fun tonight. I picked up my Nokia phone and texted Abby. I think that was her name. But it didn't matter, I just wanted an hour or two.

Thirty minutes later, I laid on the small bed in Abby's dorm room. My pants were around my ankles and Abby was on her knees, her mouth wrapped around my dick. Just the way I liked it too. She had definitely improved since the last time I saw her. This night was getting better and better.

I closed my eyes, relishing the fact that I was close to busting a nut and then I could be deep inside of her until I was done. And while that didn't seem like that would be a big deal to anyone else that wasn't me. I didn't care.

She made a noise with her mouth, and I grunted. God damn, this was good. I felt my dick throb in her mouth as I let loose cursing under my breath. Sure, I could've warned her that I was coming, but then again at the moment I didn't care. And by the way, she was lapping it all up, I really didn't think she cared.

After that, she stood up and smiled.

"So you ready for round two?" she said with a wide grin on her face.

"Fuck yeah I am," I said, getting up and throwing her on the bed.

I was more than ready.

Chapter Four

Leah

I groaned as I made my way through the stands of the school stadium. Our school's football team The Vipers were about to play their first game of the season. For some reason, Marcy thought it would be okay to drag me here with her because she reported the sports stories for the school's newspaper. I knew also that it had to do with the fact that she was kind of seeing the QB of the football team, but she always vehemently denied that. I think something started with the two of them in our freshman year, but I couldn't be sure.

We sat in what she said was her normal seats from the year before and I prepared myself for the screams and the loud chants of the school in the stadium or as we students called it *The Pit*. This school was known for having one of the best team support systems, and no matter how appreciative I was for good ol' school spirit, I would have rather been in my room finishing up my article or reading a book. Yes, I was one of the girls who loved books. Loved them.

Our team was doing great, and I watched as the school got pumped as the team scored another touchdown. Marcy was jumping up and down and I was sure it was because of the player wearing the number 10. He was the QB. I found myself drawn to the big guy with the dark hair, wearing a jersey with the number 47. I think he was a linebacker. And he was doing his thing. He already sacked the quarterback from Miami University.

By the last few seconds of the game, I couldn't help, but be caught up in everyone else's excitement. This was a damn good game. The kind of game that had you clutching at your chest, hoping that the team pulled off the win. It was much too close. When the seconds ticked down to zero, everyone cheered and it sounded like the cheers of those in a rock concert happy to be a part of it all.

"Oh my God! How exciting was that? Like this was freaking amazing," Marcy said. She grabbed my hand. "Come with me." I grabbed my bag and followed her through the crowd until we reached the sidelines where the team was.

I could see the QB Tommy Allen eyeing Marcy and he ran over to her. Tommy was a blond, blue-eyed god. He was very handsome. I could see the appeal and why Marcy may have been smitten.

"Thanks for being here," he said to her and pulled her into a hug. I smiled at that because it was sweet. And after dealing with my parent's constant disappointment in my college choices, I could use all the lovey-dovey stuff I could get. It was a nice change of pace.

Once they pulled apart, Marcy turned towards me.

"Tommy, this is my friend Leah. Leah, this is Tommy."

"Hey, Tommy. Nice to meet you. I've heard a lot about you," I said, trying to talk over the crowd, reaching my hand out to shake his hand.

"I've heard a lot about you as well. We don't do handshakes around here," he said, giving me a hug. I laughed.

"You're a friendly one."

"For the most part. It's nice to meet you. ."

The guy that I was watching on the field ran up to us.

"That was a great fucking game," he said loudly to Tommy.

"It was. You were great out there Adrian. As always."

Adrian. Why did he look so damn familiar? And then it hit me. He was the guy who saw me crying. The same guy who bumped into me because he was watching some girl in a skirt. He asked me was I okay, but I was angry about many things. *So, that explained why he was so damn massive.* He was a football player. And even with him standing here, I felt he took up much too space even on the football field. I couldn't tell if I liked that or not. His arms were huge and his jersey almost looked like I could see every single one of his abs.

"You were too man," he said, clapping Tommy hard on his back. He ran his hands through his hair, sweat glistening on his face.

"I'm so pumped right now, I could just kiss someone."

And as he said that, he looked at me with a curious glance on his face, and he grabbed my shoulders and placed his lips roughly on mine.

I froze momentarily shocked that it had happened. Appalled that he thought that was okay and annoyed that he thought this was a take charge kind of moment with a person he didn't even know.

I pushed my hands into his chest and he was damn near unmovable. He was a solid mass. He pulled away from me then, a cocky glance on his face.

"What the hell are you doing?" I screamed at him, embarrassed that he did that. Shaking with anger, my hands balled into tiny fists.

"Relax! It was just as a kiss."

Just a kiss! Like who the fuck did this douche think he was?

"No. It's not okay to just go up to people and kiss them, asshole."

"It's not a big deal," he said with a shrug.

I didn't know if I was still pumped from the game, or what had come over me as this wasn't my normal behavior, but I felt my right hand rise quickly and I slapped him. Hard. Or hard enough for me. "Save that shit for someone else. Because I'm not one of the bimbos you're probably used to."

He held his face, with a mix of shock and amusement on his face. And then he gave that cocky grin that became a signature of his.

"Most girls would die to kiss me."

"Adrian, right? I'm not most girls. You're not that damn special. You're an ass. Truly." And with that, I spun around and walked away. Sure, I felt bad for slapping him. I knew it wasn't okay to do that, but I also felt in a way he had it coming. Who just came up to people and do that anyway? *Stupid fucking jock.*

I would apologize to Marcy later for leaving. But I had to get away from this sports stuff. I had to get back to my apartment. And away from that football player named Adrian.

But, boy how wrong I was in thinking that would be the last time I would have to interact with him.

Chapter Five

Adrian

A few weeks later Tommy and I made my way to the bar that

was hosting a party for the football team. It was the usual

thing to do after the win. Our team was on a roll, and what

better way was it than to celebrate another win. Besides, we

would be on the road for the two next weeks. Tommy was

driving and I was in the passenger seat as the music flowed

from the car's speakers. I was all too ready to party and have a

good time. We arrived fifteen minutes later and it was

crowded. Making our way through the crowd, we found other

team members sitting at the table. Plopping down, I grabbed a

beer and took a swig from the bottle feeling good and happy

that I would be able to relieve a little bit of tension and stress.

The season was always something that could make or break a person depending on what year you was on the team.

Moments later a cute blonde sat on my lap and leaned in whispering in my ear. She wanted to fuck. And who was I to tell a girl who was willing, no?

Tommy sat down next to me and shook his head. He was a goody two shoes. Though I expected it had to do with that girl Mary…no Marcy. That was her name. She was a cute brunette so I did see why he was so interested in her. That's when I saw the little minx from our first game of the season. I was high on the win and I kissed her. She had phenomenal lips too. Full with just enough room for me to bite on them and tug on them. Instead of her wanting to take it further, she slapped me. She slapped me pretty good too. I haven't seen her since then, and her friend Marcy and Tommy gave me shit about it. I didn't think it was that serious though. It was just a kiss. Nothing more. It wasn't like I fucked her or anything, but Tommy said Marcy wouldn't let it go, and so he had to say something. I was almost sure it was because her friend was still pissed. What was her name again, anyway?

I saw Marcy talking to her, but the girl seemed annoyed more than anything. I was tempted to go over to her, but I also wanted the girl in my lap. Besides, if I got into a spat with anyone, it may ruin my chances of getting lucky and I couldn't have that. I had a lot of stress to release.

Marcy headed towards our table, and once she saw me, her once friendly expression changed into a scowl.

"What are you doing here?" she asked, with her hands on her hips.

"Uh, my team is here and so am I," I said amused. I give her that she was a loyal friend. Marcy rolled her eyes and sat on Tommy's lap, leaning into him. I was sure they would be leaving soon, and that would be my cue to get this woman on my lap more of my attention. The girl put my hand on her breast whispering things into my ear.

However, I found myself watching Marcy's friend. I admit she didn't act like how the other girls did around me and that intrigued me. Most girls would do anything to say they fucked me, but she didn't seem at all amused or even cared about who I was. I saw a guy talking to her and I pushed the girl off and stood up.

"Sorry," I mumbled. Who the fuck was this prick? And who did he think he was trying to talk to her? I found myself moving toward her.

"Get off of me," I heard her say loudly, and I strode over there quickly grabbing the guy's arm who had his hand wrapped around hers.

"I think she said, to let her go," I said, my voice dangerously low.

The guy turned around and I could tell that already he was drunk. He looked me up and down, sizing me up. He probably was trying to see if he could take me. I did the same. I knew from looking at him that I could take him. He looked at her again and then back and me before jerking himself out of my grip.

"Alright man. You got it. She's way too uptight anyway," he said before stumbling off.

I could see she was flustered and angry.

"Are you okay?" I asked her genuinely concerned, my voice unnaturally soft.

"Yeah. I'm fine. Thanks. You know I could've handled him though," she said.

"I'm sure."

"No. Seriously. I had it. It wasn't a big deal."

"I know. You seemed to have handled me just fine."

She seemed confused for a second and then she laughed.

"Oh yeah. Sorry about that. I don't normally resort to violence, but you kinda had it coming."

"Yeah. I can't argue that. I definitely did. I was happy and you were there…"

"And you just kiss random girls?"

"Yes and no."

"Hmm. That's how you catch stuff."

"You know you can't catch anything from kissing right?"

"Obviously I didn't mean anything like that. I was being sarcastic. But then again, I'm sure with all the things in the world, you can."

I laughed.

"So, what's your name again?"

"That many girls huh? Guess, it's hard to keep up with someone who doesn't particularly like you."

"No. I just couldn't remember after you slapped me. You slapped me so hard I think you knocked a couple of screws loose." I chuckled.

"You are definitely exaggerating. It's Leah."

"Leah. Nice! I'm Adrian. It's nice to meet you properly," I said, reaching out my hand to shake hers.

She looked at my hand suspiciously, before placing her hand in mine and shaking it. Her hand was warm and so small. My hand practically swallowed hers.

The girl who was on my lap came over to me.

"And now that you're done playing hero, can we have a little fun?" she asked me eyeing Leah and glaring at her.

Leah looked between the two of us, a look of disdain on her face, and she moved.

"You two have fun," she said before walking back over to where Tommy and Marcy sat.

I was at a loss for words, as she walked away.

"Who was that?" the girl in front of me asked. I still didn't know her name.

"It doesn't matter," I replied nonchalantly.

Shrugging, she grabbed my dick.

"How about we take this someplace else?" she whispered.

A big part of me wanted to take her up on that offer. But for some unknown reason, another part of me wanted to talk to Leah.

"Maybe later," I said flippantly, removing her hand. I made it back to the table and smirked.

"So, you decided we weren't losers after all?" I asked, trying to lighten the scowl that was on her face.

"I'm talking to Marcy and Tommy. You? Well, you just happened to be here. Or happen to be anywhere I seem to be."

She made a face that screamed annoyed and sighed.

"I'm about to head out. This really isn't my scene," Leah said to Marcy.

"You want me to walk you back?" I asked quickly.

All of them looked at me.

"No, I'm good. I can probably catch a cab if I really need to."

"It's late and there are other guys who probably feel the way that guy that grabbed you do. I am walking you back to your dorm. End of story."

I had put my foot down, though I didn't know why I felt the sudden urge to make sure she was okay. Safe. That I needed to make sure no one else touched her. She was definitely different than the other girls and I had to admit I kind of liked it.

"I don't live in the dorms. And, I don't need you or want you to walk me home!"

58

"You don't really have a choice."

"Who the hell do you think you are? You don't get to tell me what I can and cannot do. I don't need your permission to go home."

I groaned. "Must you be so difficult? I didn't say that. I would just feel a lot better if you let me walk you back."

"Why does it matter?"

I didn't know what to say to that, so instead, I just shrugged.

She exhaled deeply.

"Fine. Let me just use the bathroom."

I nodded as she went off to the bathroom. I kept my gaze in the direction she went, my eyes darting between the bathroom door and Tommy. Marcy sat on his lap, the two of them locked in a kiss. And I had to admit watching the two of them go at it made me tempted to take that girl up on her offer at all. The other part of me wanted to make sure Leah got home safe. That, and she intrigued me. She was a firecracker and a bit of a mystery all wrapped in one.

"Okay, I'm ready," Leah said as she approached me.

"I was sure you escaped out the bathroom window or something."

"I considered it," she replied with a smirk.

Marcy looked between the two of us concern on her face.

"Are you sure, you don't want me to go with you? It's not a problem," Marcy said, suspicion marking her soft features.

"I'll walk with her," I said.

Tommy had an expression on his face that I couldn't read, but he nodded.

"Okay, Leah. If you're sure, I will probably be back a little late," Marcy said, ignoring what I felt she wanted to say.

"Yep. I got it. Ciao love," Leah said, turning around. "Let's go!"

I followed her out of the bar and we walked up the street heading back towards where she lived. The noise began to die down the further we walked. There was nothing but the sounds of our steps and I found myself lost for words, wanting to ask her things, wanting to know more about her. But for some reason I was afraid and I didn't know why that was. I was usually the in your face kind of guy. As I walked with her, I debated striking up a conversation. I didn't want to say something stupid and her getting mad. I went against my better judgment and asked anyway.

"How come I've never seen you on campus before the night I bumped into you?" I asked.

"I live in the apartments next to the University. I'm only on campus for my classes and the school's paper."

"Nice. I should've done that, but I think my mom kind of likes me not living at home, but also likes that she can keep an eye on me at the dorms."

"Oh," she said not seeming too concerned.

"I still feel like I've should've seen you more though," I said.

"We don't hang in the same circles."

"Meaning?"

"You're this enormous football jock, and I'm the girl obsessed with books and good grades. I like to write and report on things, and you like to be rough on the football field. That is probably the most basic way to describe that."

"You think I'm enormous?"

"Look at you and look at me. I'm small in size and standing next to you makes me look like a child."

"I don't know any child who can slap like you do."

She laughed.

"Well, I beg to differ. But I'm just saying that you are a football player and you make me look like a china doll," she said.

"You think all I do is be rough on the field?"

She stopped walking and turned towards me. "Am I wrong?"

"Yes! My position is important on the field. All of us are. We have to work like a machine, all together, so we can win. It is what any football player does. At least a good one."

She cocked her head slightly, but then shrugged her shoulders. "I guess."

"You guess? What does that even mean?"

"It means exactly what I said. I'm not an athlete, so you're not going to see me make any reference to what I don't know. I leave all the sports stuff to Marcy. She follows all of that. She lives for sports. I have more important things to worry about."

"So sports isn't important?"

"To me? No! Sure, it gets people together and it requires team effort most of the time, but sports is just that. Sports! It isn't going to stop the shitty things that happen."

"And you think shitty things wouldn't happen if there weren't any sports?"

"I didn't say that."

"So, what are you saying?"

"Nothing. It doesn't matter."

"Yeah. It does. So tell me."

"Why are you asking so many questions?"

"I'm just curious about you." I glanced at her then, her face locked in a grimace.

We started walking again, and I followed her lead. Her hands were tightly clenched on the straps of her purse almost as if she was mad about something.

"Some of you athletes think you are above the rules. The law, whatever. Some of you feel that you are something so special that you should have certain standards that don't apply to you. Personally, it sickens me. I know it isn't all of you, but it is enough of you. All the passes, you get because you're on the team. If you play a good game of a sport. Fine do that. But don't think it is supposed to excuse you from bad behavior. Or those who have to get partnered up with you athletes who don't want to actually do your coursework. It's aggravating. Like we have to save you so you can get a passing grade, while you can skate by on the sole fact that you know how to do something with a ball."

I nodded in deep thought. She may have had a point. She sped up her pace so I ran to catch up to her.

You're putting us all in one box. How can you be so sure that all athletes behave that way? "You make it quite easy. You've done nothing to prove me wrong."

64

I laughed.

"You're right. But most of us play sports because we love it. We love winning. We love the adrenaline rush you get when you put your all into something. Sometimes is an outlet to get away from things that are bothering us or getting to us. We aren't all jerks."

"Is that your personal testament? Because you did come off as a jerk the first time I've ever had contact with you. Actually, you were an ass. And if I had been in a better frame of mind at the point I probably would've punched you rather than slapped you."

I chuckled, running my hand through my hair. "The very first time we met. And it was an accident. I didn't mean to bump into you."

"Maybe if you weren't staring at that girl's cleavage you would've seen me walking there."

"True. I'm sorry about that."

"And then the very next time you kiss me like I know you or something. That's a behavior of yours? Kissing random girls?"

"I'm sorry about that too. I wasn't thinking. I'm used to girls not having a problem with that. It won't happen again. I promise."

"Don't make promises you can't keep."

"I don't know if I should take it as a challenge or a warning," I said with a chuckle.

She shook her head, amused. "It was a warning. Let that happen again and I will kick you in your stuff down there."

"My stuff down there?"

"You know what I mean."

"No, I don't," I said. I kind of liked that she was getting flustered. It was different than what I've seen before. I liked it.

"Your dick! The head you seem to like to think with the most. "

"I know what you meant. I just wanted you to say that. And are you always this mean?"

"No. You seem to bring out the worse in me. The absolute worst."

I laughed loudly then and she looked at me, her brow furrowed with frustration.

"I do? I don't know you enough to do that."

"You are a typical guy with an asshole complex, that doesn't require a need to know you for a long time."

"Okay, maybe sometimes I'm an asshole. But not always."

"And you're cocky too."

"I'll admit to that. But for you, I'll try not to be that way. Or limit it. If you'd allow that."

"What do you think we're going to be best friends? That we're going to be pals and do all these interesting things together? You are incredibly bold. I'll give you that."

"Wow. You don't think we can be friends?"

"No. I don't. Again, we are from two different worlds. We are two different people and people like us shouldn't be friends. That's all there is to it."

There was silence again, but I continued to stare at her. She was opinionated and feisty. I liked it. It was a major turn on. And she was really pretty. She had cat shaped eyes and

67

high cheekbones. Her body was a bit on the slim side, but she still had some meat on her in all the right places. I liked it a whole lot. And I admit that I really wanted to see if I could change her mind about me.

By the time we reached her apartment building, I realized I didn't want to leave her just yet. She turned towards me.

"Well, thank you for walking me back. You didn't have to. But thanks."

"What kind of a gentleman would I be if I didn't?"

"Gentleman? Uh, I guess the same kind of guy you were before you met me I suppose."

"Ouch. That hurts," I said, placing my hand on my chest in mock despair.

She laughed, shaking her head.

"Sure, buddy. I'm going to shower and go to sleep. I have to finish a paper anyway. Maybe you're not so bad after all. Or maybe you are. Who knows?"

"I take that as a win for now. Good night, Leah."

"Good night."

She opened the door, waved and closed it and I turned back around. I thought about going back to the bar, but I was too wound up now. And for some reason, I wanted to imagine her. Imagine her hands all over me. My hands touching her in places no one has ever touched her.

And as easy as it would be to have sex with someone, I didn't. Instead, I walked back to the dorms, and to my room. Plopping down on my bed, I unzipped my pants and grabbed my dick. It was hard as a rock. There was no way I would be able to relax if I didn't get off. Gripping it tightly, I thought of Leah's full lips around it. I closed my eyes, picturing her on top of me, her beautiful brown skin glowing, her breasts bouncing freely and her eyes closed as she moved up and down my shaft. I groaned again as I stroked myself to her image, picturing what she looked like under her clothes. I could feel my orgasm building up and I let out a sound I didn't recognize, as I came. My hand stayed on my dick until I let everything out.

I sat up looking at the mess and grinned. Leah had me beating off to her, and she didn't even have to do anything to get my attention. But she did. She was feisty and beautiful.

And even better I already had a taste of her full lips. I wasn't

going to stop until I could taste them again. Or until I could

have all of her on top of me or underneath me.

Chapter Six

Leah

I finished my last article for the paper and shut down the computer. I had a long day and I was ready to go back home and relax. I could get some snacks and pig out. Maybe even watch a movie or two.

"Hey, Leah, Tommy is going to this party later and he wanted me to ask you to come. Would you be down?" Marcy said coming into the room where I was.

I sighed. "Do I really have to go?" I asked.

"No. But I would appreciate it and it should be fun. You and I both know that we had a hard week and we need to let loose a little. And they will be leaving tomorrow to go on the road. We should let our hair down and relax."

"You know I can do that at home right? I don't really need to go to a party." I said with my brow raised.

"No! That would be boring and we are two pretty college girls that have good grades and need a fun night or two once in a while. You really need to learn how to loosen up a little Leah. We are young. You have plenty of time to stay home and watch movies or sulk for whatever reason," she said with disdain.

"And what is that supposed to mean?" I said, annoyed at her and at this conversation.

"I didn't mean it the way it sounds. Just that I want to have fun with you, and yes, Tommy will be there, but I want to hang out with you. Girl time and fun! I promise the next time we can hang out and watch a movie. I will even let you pick the movie," she said.

"Who has a party on a Wednesday?"

"Apparently football players."

I rolled my eyes playfully before sighing. "Fine! We can go Marcy, but that means whatever I pick you can't complain or I swear I am not going to another party with you ever again," I said with a small smile.

"Great! Let's go get ready then. Maybe you can wear that dress that you have been hiding in the closet forever," Marcy said with a wink. With a groan, I let her pull me out of the newspaper office.

Three hours later, after more complaining and going through the clothes that I had, I decided that Marcy was right, maybe I did need to wear this dress because I did spend money on it. It was a tight gray dress that showed my cleavage and shaped my hips well. For someone who was as small in stature as I was, it was rare to find something I could wear that didn't make me look like I was a kid playing dress up.

"Wow Leah, you look fantastic. You are going to be turning heads tonight!" Marcy said.

Marcy had cut her hair recently, so her hair, which was now in a bob, was semi-wet. She wore tight waist jeans and a crop top that worked with her tall frame.

"So are you darling! Let's go before I change my mind."

A cab ride and 15 bucks later, we were at the house that the party was taking place. Apparently one of the guys on the football team parents were out of town and he was using it as an excuse to throw a big party. We walked into the house and there were people all over the place. I already felt confined and wanted to leave.

"Hey ladies!" Tommy said coming up to us and placing his arms around our shoulders. "I'm glad you made it. It wouldn't have been the same without the two of you."

I raised an eyebrow because it was clear he was stretching it a bit with what he said. Marcy, on the other hand, was eating it up and I didn't want to dash her hopes because she was so happy about Tommy. I hoped the two of them made it throughout the football and after college, because from what I saw he made her happy.

One of my favorite dance songs came on and Marcy gave me the look. We were about to show them how we got down when it came to dancing. We moved to the beat, our hips moving in the same motion, and we danced with each other. I had to admit that Marcy was right. I was having fun, and I was letting loose. I haven't done that in a while. My homework would still be there once I get back. Five songs later, I went to the kitchen to get me something to drink. I was parched and my feet were starting to hurt. I regretted wearing the heels, I chose to wear with this dress. Making my way around the house, I saw that Marcy was dancing with Tommy. I took that as my cue to go find someplace to sit for a bit and rest my feet.

I walked down the hallway to find a place to sit and bumped into some girl with curly red hair.

"I'm sorry," I said apologetically.

"It's okay," she said and then I watched as she made her way to none other than Adrian. Of course, he would be here. Why would I expect otherwise when the party was being thrown by one of his teammates. The house was huge, which explained why I didn't see him before.

He took her and pinned her against the wall, feeling up on her and I found myself looking at him with disgust as his hands roamed the girl's breasts. Fuming, I brushed past them as I walked by. Did I really need to be subjected to this kind of behavior? And why did it piss me off so much?

I needed to get some air and away from that asshole. This seemed to be his normal behavior and it pissed me off. It shouldn't have. It was irrational. He was nothing to me. And yet, here I was angry.

Once I finally got to the balcony, I sat on the small couch, soda in my hand and looked out at the grounds of the house. The lawn and flowers were beautifully manicured. It was a nice change from all the chaos that was at that party.

Here I was a college-aged girl at a party that was actually pretty fun, and yet here I sat alone on the balcony. I knew if Marcy knew this is where I snuck off to, she would be upset. The music was loud and I wanted a moment to breathe, even if it was only just a moment. Maybe I was too uptight. And didn't know how to have fun. But this was how I always was. I kept to myself and focused on my studies.

"Hey," I heard a deep voice say. And without looking up I already knew it was Adrian. As it seemed to be the norm for him, his presence took over the area, and I glanced up at him before looking back at the lawn.

"Shouldn't you be with your plaything right about now?" I asked dryly.

"Who? Bella? She isn't my plaything. It was just a little fun. Nothing more."

"I see. That whole it was just a little fun seem to be your theme. Maybe you should go back inside and stick to it. I want to be alone right now," I said.

Ignoring me he sat next to me, invading my nose with his scent, and invading my personal space by being much too close. Much too close for comfort.

"I guess I don't speak English," I said loudly, hoping Adrian would take the hint, but he ignored me again.

"Why are you out here anyway?"

"I wanted to be alone and rest my feet," I said.

Adrian looked down at my feet and smirked.

"Sounds like you were having fun."

"Oh, so you did see me?"

"Yeah. I did."

"And still…"

"Still what?" he asked.

But I didn't answer it. I couldn't. Because I knew I had no right to be upset with him.

"Anyway, I was dancing. I wasn't having your kind of fun."

"Who says I wasn't dancing," he asked.

"Your tongue seemed to be down the throat of the girl whose breasts were in your hands, but whatever you say."

Adrian laughed then. It was deep and it both made me curious and irked me at the same time. I didn't think that was even possible. But Adrian seemed to be one of those guys who made me feel things that didn't make sense. He also couldn't take a hint. He wouldn't go away no matter what you did.

"Can I touch your feet?"

"Excuse me?" I said, my voice on edge.

"I'm going to rub your feet. You said they were bothering you, and I didn't want to just touch them without your permission."

I laughed.

"Why would you want to rub my feet? That sounds a bit forward."

"I thought I'd be nice. Your feet are hurting, and my hands are available. A win for you if you look at the bigger picture."

"Oh, so now you have some manners?" I said my brow raised.

"I'm trying to," he said.

Cautiously, I placed my feet on his lap. He took my right foot first, and his strong hands worked some magic. I let out a slight moan solely based on the fact that it felt good.

"I think I like the way that sounds," he said quietly, his tone not sounding the way it was before.

"I'm sorry. My feet were killing me and your hands are super strong. It feels great," I replied quickly.

Adrian nodded. His hands felt perfect. He took the other foot into his hands doing the same as before.

"You know you look beautiful in that dress," he said.

"I bet you say that to all the girls," I scoffed.

"I might say things to benefit me in the long run, but I don't tell all girls that they are beautiful. Those kinds of things should be reserved for special people."

"You just called me beautiful. Why? I don't think I'm that special."

"Maybe you are."

I didn't know what to say to him after that. It was strange, the things I was feeling. Part of me was still annoyed by the shit I saw in the hallway, and the other half of me did like that he was sitting here with me and rubbing my feet.

"Thank you," I said quietly, moving the hair out of my face.

He stopped rubbing my feet and I placed them back in my heels.

"You came here with Marcy?" he asked.

"Yeah. She was the reason I decided to come to this party in the first place. She thought that it would be fun. And it was for the most part."

"What are your plans after this?"

"I am going to crash in my bed and sleep."

"Are you always this boring?" he asked, his playful tone slipping back into place.

"I guess. I get that some think college is this place to party, but I have plans, and college is my way to get them. It is the reason that I work so hard and try to keep up with my grades. I don't want anything in my way," I said honestly. I stood up and he followed suit.

"I get that. But you have to enjoy life too or it will pass you by and before you know it, you will be regretting that you didn't stop, take a moment and let it all in."

Again, I was a bit lost for words. I have had many people say the same thing. That life was much too short and that I should enjoy it. Even my parents agreed with that analogy, even if they didn't agree with my career choice. But yet, I always found myself holding back. Maybe it was fear. Fear of the unknown. Fear of letting go without having any control over things or rather trusting things even if I couldn't control them.

We stood there looking at each other. I felt something I've never felt before and it coiled in my stomach. For a moment the loud music from inside seemed muffled. I could see a difference in his eyes this time, not the usual amusement that danced in them. It was almost as it time as stilled.

I stared at him, his hair a bit unruly, and his expression serious. He was right, but I wasn't going to tell him that. He was cocky enough, and I wasn't good at giving compliments to guys, especially when they were like him. Sexy, aggravating and a playboy kind of guy. He cleared his throat, and the feeling between us passed as quickly as it had come. Maybe I can give the one being friends thing a shot. Instead of saying all those things. I only said one.

"Do you want to dance?"

Chapter Seven

Adrian

We made our way back to the dance floor, my hand in hers.

She wasn't mad at me. She wasn't cursing or yelling and she asked me to dance. Who was I to turn her down? I loved the way the dress she wore fit all parts of her frame, and once again I wondered how she looked under it. Wondered if I could make her moan the way she did on the balcony.

Usher's "Yeah" came on and she smiled as she danced with me. I could feel her ass pressed against me as she grinded to the song, and I wanted her more than I've ever wanted anything before, but I kept my cool. I danced not saying what I wanted and not putting my foot in my mouth.

There was a certain part of the song came on and she danced close to me. Much too close. I could feel my dick getting hard, and I had to give myself space from her. She was playing in dangerous territory now and I had to remember not to say things that I would normally say or normally do to get a girl in bed with me. Usually, I didn't have to say much. Being on the football team was enough. But with Leah, it was different. I couldn't do that without knowing she was going to put me in my place if I even came to her like that.

"Leah, you are killing me right now," I whispered into her ear as I spun her around.

"It's just dancing. Nothing more. Nothing less," she said, her voice not sounding as convincing as her words.

Marcy had waved at Leah and Leah smiled, telling her to come over.

"Ah, so I see you found Leah, Adrian. I was looking for her," she said.

"We were just talking and dancing," I said, running my hands through my hair. I was partially grateful for the interruption as it gave me a chance to calm down and give myself a pep talk.

Leah gave me a strange look, but didn't say anything.

"I was trying to enjoy myself, which you insisted that I do. But here I am. Is something wrong?" Leah asked.

"No. I just thought maybe you used the separation as a cue to go home," Marcy replied.

"You think I'm that bad?" Leah said with a small pout.

Marcy laughed. "Uh, yeah. You don't know how to relax and have fun. I get it. I do, but sometimes we all need to wind down a little. That's all. But even if you are too stubborn, I love you. And I got your back. Even if it means protecting you from pigheaded jerks like this one," Marcy said pointing towards me.

I mockingly feigned hurt. I knew I was being an asshole before, but I was interested in this girl. More interested than I've ever been in anyone before.

"Who me?"

"Yes, you Adrian. Be a better guy and I wouldn't have to say those kinds of things.

Raising my hands in defense, I laughed lightly.

"You got it, Marcy. I promise to try and be on my best behavior. I know how close the two of you are, but maybe I'm not as bad as you think," I said sincerely.

Leah looked at me, but I stared at Marcy hoping that she could believe that I was interested in the sassy girl who wanted to be a journalist. Tommy glanced between the two of us before breaking the silence.

"Okay, then let's get back to partying, the night is young," he said.

"Agreed," I said, grabbing Leah's hand and we continued to dance. We danced together for a while and when she tried to break away because a slow song came on, I held her to me watching her look at everything else, but at me.

"Do you always look away from people that are right in front of your face?"

She shrugged. "No. Not really. If I do, there's usually a reason. Being uncomfortable, worried, or nervous," she said.

"I make you uncomfortable or nervous?"

"No. You don't actually. It's just…you're overwhelming. You're a bit much and I don't know how to handle you. It's hard to explain."

"You seemed to have explained it just fine to me."

"Yeah. I don't know. You seem like you would be hard to contain.

"I think that can be a good thing."

"How so?"

"Well, it's not boring to want to know about things that you can't explain. Life should be exciting, and if you feel overwhelmed, just take a deep breath and breathe it all in."

Leah raised her eyebrow at me with a skeptical look on her face. "So, I'm supposed to breathe you all in?"

"No. Well, not exactly. If you think I'm too much, just slowly take it in."

"And what if I don't want to take it all in?"

I laughed. "If not would you be standing here with me spending all your time dancing with me?"

"Maybe I'm being nice."

"Or maybe you like me and don't want to admit it. It's fine though. You don't have to. I know you feel something and for that, I will stick around. I'm going to be around so much you won't be able to get me out of your mind."

"Or maybe I am passing the time slowly because I have nothing better to do."

"You don't seem to be the type of woman who would waste her time doing anything she didn't want to."

"True."

I could smell her scent, almost like cocoa butter and something else. And I inhaled her restraining myself from kissing her again.

"Can we maybe do lunch or something?"

"I'm sure we will see each other around campus."

"Maybe I want a more sure thing. More than seeing you around campus."

"Why?"

"Because honestly, I like being around you even if your face is always in a scowl."

"If that is your way of flirting you need to try a different approach."

"Am I wrong?" I asked with a smug look on my face.

"Yes! Again, you seem to bring the worse out of me."

I didn't want to seem like I was begging her.

I stopped dancing with her, to hold her gaze. "How about this? Once I get you back to your apartment, we'll exchange numbers and I'll call you. And if I don't annoy you too much then we can do lunch?"

She bit her lip, her nostrils flaring a bit as she was contemplating. Nodding softly, she leaned back in, and we continued to dance to the slow song that was different than the one that played before. I couldn't deny that I was happy, that she didn't pull away. She let me hold her in my arms, and even if it was only a small step, I was content. It was enough for now.

Chapter Eight

Leah

Two weeks later from the night Adrian walked me home, we sat in the living room of our apartment in front of the tv. We as in me, Marcy, and Tommy. While it was a small apartment, it was cozy. It was one of the things I loved about it. We sat on the couch, watching one of my favorite movies of all time. Titanic. And just as we got to see Jack all dressed in his tux, there was a knock on the door.

Marcy looked over at me and stood up to answer it. Opening the door, she shook her head.

"Hey, Adrian," she said reluctantly.

"Hey, is Tommy here?"

"Yeah. We're just watching a movie."

"Cool," he said coming in and sitting down next to me.

He didn't say anything to me, and that pissed me off. Actually, I was pissed off because two weeks had passed and he hadn't called. I understand he had practice and road games and school work, but one call doesn't take that long. Hell, even an email would've sufficed. And then he had the nerve to come into my apartment, and not say hi. I wanted to smack his stupid face. But I kept my cool, keeping my eyes on the tv. I would not get mad. This was my time to relax.

There was a good silence as the movie continued, my eyes partially misty as it always was when I watched this movie.

"I don't get how women can watch this movie and not see how fake this all is. Not, the Titanic story, but Jack and Rose are fake. How can they love each other that soon? Men don't act like that," Adrian said nonchalantly interrupting the silence with a stupid comment.

I rolled my eyes. I knew it was too good to be true. All I wanted was to enjoy my downtime. With all the stuff happening with school and deadlines for the paper, I didn't have much time to do little things that kept me relaxed. But here he had to go and ruin it.

"Here you go," Marcy muttered and I knew she said it because of what my reaction was going to be.

"How do you know men don't act like that? You know all the men in the world all of a sudden?" I asked with sarcasm.

"No. I am one so I know."

"Oh, you are one, huh? Could've fooled me"

"What is that supposed to mean?" he said, his voice moving up an octave.

"Exactly what I said. What exactly about you means you are a man? Because you play football?"

"No. I'm over 18 so…"

"Yeah, and that's about it. Because men should know when they put their foot in their mouth, but for some reason, you seem to not know when you are indeed doing that."

"How am I putting my foot in my mouth?"

I laughed and shook my head.

"You have been doing so since I've met you. And frankly, it's getting tiresome."

"And you think you're some kind of picnic to be around?"

"I'm sure I'm not all the time, but I own it. I know that about me. You truly don't seem to realize that sometimes…no actually, most times you're a big asshole."

I could see him getting angry and he stood up suddenly. "Yeah. Well, maybe I like being an asshole."

"Obviously."

"Are you always like this? You act like you don't know what it means to even have a little fun. Like fun is a foreign concept or something."

"I do know how to have fun. I have fun with those I want to. You, however, weren't part of the plan."

"You guys… maybe that's enough. It's okay to agree to disagree," Tommy stated, but he stopped talking once he saw the look I shot him.

"I can feel however I want to feel in my space. I wanted to watch this movie as I planned and I was having a good time doing so. Suddenly it isn't what I wanted it to be and now I'm wrong for being mad about it?"

"They are fictional, Leah. Fake. All of it is fake. Why does that bother you so much?"

There were many words that I wanted to say. Maybe because it made me think less about my crazy course load. Maybe because sometimes it was good to get lost in the love between fictional characters. Or because maybe I wanted that for myself one day. Someone who loved me with everything. That was freaking important. Or maybe because he had the nerve to come into my apartment and not even apologize for the fact that he didn't call me or answer my calls. And most of all because I fucking liked Titanic and wanted to watch it. I didn't think it was too crazy to ask for.

"Marcy and I do this when we can. We hang out and watch movies. Today just happened to be the day we watched Titanic. We watch movies we have seen already all the time. You two weren't supposed to be here. And while I usually make an exception for Tommy because he gets it, I didn't ask you nor want you to be here. It is like you are just the bane of

95

my existence. I don't know why you have to be such a pain in the ass, but oh my God, I don't think you even realize that you do the annoying shit that you do. It might work for all those other groupie girls that you seem to have hanging onto your every word, but I will not deal with that shit. I will not. I don't care. I will watch whatever the hell I want to watch in my apartment."

I was defiant and angry, my hands on my hips, and my nose flaring. I didn't know why he got such a reaction out of me, but I was livid. He had to know that there were plenty of jocks that looked like him. Plenty of jocks that acted like him. He was a dime a dozen.

"Well, maybe if you acted like those girls, you would get laid. It'll probably help you relax a little. You seriously need to take a chill pill. You should never be this damn upset about anything. But especially not about a movie. So, what I made a stupid comment? What else is new? I say what I feel at the moment. That's it. This isn't that serious for you to be this mad. I mean what man does what he does for Rose? She didn't even share the damn wooden door with her. She could have at least done that. People don't love like that. It isn't real. It just isn't."

Granted, he was right about Rose. I had my feelings about that, but that whole needing to get laid comment set my blood boiling and I clenched my fists realizing that maybe I was getting too heated and that it wasn't that serious, but I couldn't help it. He knew how to push all the wrong buttons and I hated it. Mostly I didn't like that most of this was because he didn't call me.

Marcy stood up. She got between the two of us. I could see her eyes pleading with me not to go where I was going to go, but I shook my head.

"Leah, he isn't worth it. Don't even worry about it. We know why we love this movie. It is the same reason why I love *A Walk to Remember*. We don't need to explain it," she said softly.

But it didn't matter because I was upset. I have never been this upset before. Or maybe I have, but I knew me and I wasn't letting this go without the last word. It wasn't in me to let things go. I always had to have the final say so and so I did.

"Listen, none of us asked you to be here. I honestly don't know why you decided to stroll in here like you own the place. Why do you always have to say something that makes no sense? Or rather say something as if that is going to magically change the other person's mind about what it is they want to do with their downtime. You always have to try and play this big, tough guy who has no emotions and use humor to downplay that maybe you aren't as great as a person as you pretend to be. Maybe all you're really good for is whatever you do on the football field and that is it. Maybe that is why you have to say the stupid stuff that comes out of your mouth. Maybe you have all those women falling all over themselves because you play football. It certainly isn't because of your personality because let's face it, it fucking sucks. Sure, you had some good moments. I'll give you that. But, normally you suck. And maybe you know that and that is why you are a pain. I don't know nor while I try to figure it out. I am over you and this conversation. You could've just been quiet and watched the damn movie like regular people do. But no! You just had to say something. Maybe I have a stick up my ass as you say because of guys like you. All the same things. All the

damn time. Unemotional, jackasses who are only good for sex

maybe. Nothing more. And I would rather have that stick so

far up my ass then ever be like that. So, now since you ruined

this day for me, I am going to my room and I am going to

relax some other way. Sorry Marcy, but I can't. It was great to

see you, Tommy."

I shook my head, trying to stop any tears from falling

down my face. Whenever I got really angry I cried and I hated

it. I hated that he was even able to get me to this point or that I

couldn't reel it in. If Tommy wasn't such a good guy to

Marcy, I would've avoided all football players like the damn

plague.

Plopping down on my bed, I closed my eyes, the hot

tears zigzagging down my face. I shouldn't have gotten this

upset about a movie, but then again, Adrian irritated me. And I

knew it had to do with the fact that he didn't keep his promise.

I didn't even know why not receiving a call from him bothered

me so much. We were friends. Or trying to be friends. But

there was something else. I wasn't ready to admit it yet. At least not out loud. *Ugh!*

I looked up at the ceiling, knowing that I would have some explaining to do with Marcy. And moments later she walked in and sat down next to me on my bed.

"Are you okay?" she asked me softly.

"Yeah. I'm fine. He just gets under my skin. But I'm fine. I'm sorry I probably ruined our movie day," I said sincerely.

"You didn't. It should've been just us girls anyway. I have a hard time telling Tommy no. He's just so cute," Marcy said with a laugh.

"He is. It's fine. I know how much you like Tommy. And we can do this again next week. You enjoy the rest of your afternoon with Tommy. I'm fine. Promise."

Marcy looked at me with a small smile. "Okay, Leah. We will chat later."

I waved to her as she made her way to the door. Closing my eyes, I thought about the exchange between Adrian and me. Perhaps I was much too hard on him. I knew that's how I was when I was angry. My mouth was one to be reckoned with. Not that I haven't tried to get better with what I let come out my mouth when I was pissed, but it had a mind of its own and I would be left holding the carnage of what I said. Adrian was probably pissed off, not that he didn't deserve to be because I was angry too. But still, the nice part of me felt terrible that I was so mean. Sighing, I sat back up. Maybe he was back in his dorm room. I could go over there and apologize. Only for the fact that what I said came out so mean.

Opening the door to my room, I made my way back to the living room and saw that Adrian was still sitting there with his eyes closed. Why didn't he leave when Marcy and Tommy did? I took a few deep breaths, trying to control my emotions. If I didn't it would defeat the whole conversation I had with myself to apologize to him.

"You're still here?" I asked him instead.

He opened his eyes and looked at me. A range of emotion passing over his strong features. He seemed in deep thought. What I couldn't truly be sure. But his face went from anger to hurt and then impassive.

101

"Yeah. I wanted to apologize to you. I know I pushed your buttons and I felt that I needed to at least say I was sorry."

"Oh."

"I've seen you mad before. But today seemed more than usual. And while normally I would've been like fuck it. For some reason, I couldn't leave until I apologized."

I contemplated his words. So we were on the same page? Both of us want to apologize for this argument that really shouldn't have happened in the first place.

"I want to apologize as well. I know I can be a bit much sometimes. Growing up in my family, it is kind of hard not to always be on the defense with things. But I crossed the line and I said some things that I shouldn't have said. I know how my mouth is when I'm pissed, and I took it too far. I'm sorry."

There was silence as I watched him look at me, his gaze intense. He ran his fingers through his hair and then abruptly stood up. He made his way to me and I found myself trying to figure out what was it about him that got me so riled up. I watched his strong jaw as he studied me and found

myself glancing at his lips and then his shoulders. They were

strong. Really strong and it worried me. It worried me a lot.

Not that it was bad, but that maybe even if it was only for a

moment, I wouldn't mind his strong arms around me again.

And I didn't know why that thought crossed my mind because

I had no time for relationships especially a guy like him. It

was only in the cards that I would be hurt. And I didn't want

to be hurt. I didn't want that kind of stress. I just needed to

finish school.

"Leah, you are… I don't know how to explain it. But I

can't keep my mind off of you. Believe me, I tried. As soon as

you slapped me that day after the game, I told myself that I

didn't need a girl like you around me. There would always be

other girls. Hell, I always told myself that. It's easier that way.

I tried telling myself that there were plenty of girls who

wouldn't slap me or only would slap me if we were in bed

together. Yet, I find myself here waiting for you to come out

of your room so I can apologize. I know I make you mad. I

know I'm a jerk sometimes. Usually I don't care what other

people think of me, I do care when it comes to you. Sure, I joke around a lot, but I know better. With the parents I have, I kind of have to. I do let the football stuff get to my head because it is the one thing I do where I don't feel like I need anyone's approval but my own. I know what I put in and I know I give it my all. It is the reason that I can do this with no issue."

He stopped shifting his foot a little. I gave a shake of my head as a sign of encouragement to continue.

"But, then there's you. Constantly on my mind and driving me crazy with your pouty lips and your high cheekbones. I keep thinking about how your lips felt on mine that night and I think to myself, that I wouldn't mind having them on me again and again. That if I have to have them again. I didn't mean it about you getting laid. I was just annoyed that you were so mad about something I didn't think was serious."

He stepped back and I found myself momentarily a loss for words. He said a mouthful, but all I could focus on was him saying to me that he couldn't keep me out of his head. That he wanted to do things to me that kind of excited me and scared me at the same time.

"Why didn't you call me? You promised me you would," I said softly.

"Is that why you were so upset with me?"

"No...maybe. Yeah."

He chuckled at that. "We had two away games and practice. And my classes. And the coach riding my ass, which he does a lot. I honestly didn't do it on purpose. I was busy."

"Too busy to at least respond and tell me that. I give you a chance and then you completely ruin it by not doing what you said."

"I only get one chance, huh?"

I glared at him.

He stepped closer. "I'm sorry. I fucked up. I fuck up a lot. I'm not good at this kind of thing Leah. I don't do whatever this is. I'm not romantic. I'm just sure of the fact that you've been driving me crazy. In all the ways that can be counted. I don't get it."

He ran his hands through his hair again. It was something he did often.

"But why? I don't get it."

"Does it really matter why? I don't know what it is about you. I just know what you make me feel. I know that I want to be around you even if you don't want to be around me. I can deal with that for now. I want to be around you. I need to be around you. Even when you're mad at me." He paused and gave a slightly sarcastic laugh. "You probably think I'm crazy, right?"

"No. I don't. I mean I don't get it, but I don't think you're crazy. Or maybe you are. Maybe we both are."

"Do you forgive me?" he asked with a shy smile on his face. It was a smile much different from the cocky one that normally graced his face. It threw me off a bit.

I nodded.

"I want all the things that I see in the movies. Like how Jack was with Rose. He loved her. All of her. I want to feel so much love that I don't know what to do with it. An epic love that defies all the odds. And it can't be nothing under that. I want it all."

"And you should have all those things," he said quietly.

He held out his hand as a sign of forgiveness, and I took it awkwardly.

"Maybe..."

"Maybe what?"

But he didn't respond. Instead, his grip tightened and in that brief pause, his stare had sharpened. I felt a pull between the two of us. I could smell his scent and it was intoxicating. And as his hand went towards my face, my breath hitched. His fingers lightly touched my cheek, heat radiating off of him. His lips brushed mine and like in a trance I responded. His mouth to mine, I felt drugged-high. Every time his tongue touched mine, it sent a shiver down my spine, and I had to stop myself. I couldn't breathe.

"I'm sorry, I didn't mean to do that," he said, his voice strained.

"Uh…don't worry about it. And I hope you can forgive me too." I tried to bring it back to why I initially came out of my room. I couldn't focus on the kiss. Or the fact that he made want to throw all caution into the wind.

His breath was heavy, and I could see his lust filled expression change as if he was trying to control what he was feeling. A part of me didn't want him to.

"I went overboard. I didn't mean all of what was said. Though sometimes you ask for it, but you know that," I said instead.

"I do."

We both laughed at that. His somewhat shaky.

"If you want, we can watch Titanic again. From the beginning. I promise I won't say anything stupid about it."

I tilted my head trying to figure out what his game was. Why would he want to watch this with me after everything that just happened?

"Um. Okay," I said, getting the remote so I can start the DVD over again. I plopped down on the couch and he sat down next to me. Close enough to make me self-conscious. I found myself wondering what he was thinking, but I was too afraid to ask him.

The movie started again and my eyes stayed glued to the television as Leo DiCaprio made his first appearance. He was one of my favorite actors, but I loved him in this movie because at the end of the day, I was a sap. I loved all that mushy stuff and the only person who really knew that was Marcy. It didn't take much for me to cry at a movie. Or wish that I could be one of those women who has a man who wants nothing but them and only them. That seemed to be a lot to ask for these days, and so I kept those kinds of thoughts to myself and stayed content with the movies I watched and the books I read.

I found myself sighing happily at some of the things that were said, and by the end of the movie, as usual, I was crying, my hands somehow entwined with his hair. His head was on my lap. I didn't know how he got there or when it happened. But it felt normal. It felt right.

"Are you okay?" he asked, somewhat amused as a tear dropped onto his cheek.

"Yes. I am. Sorry. I do this every time as if I don't know what's going to happen. I swear you think I would accept it by now, but nope I won't. I am going to be 90 years old and still not accept that Jack didn't make it to the end."

Adrian laughed, sitting up. "Well, maybe it is weird that you haven't let it go yet, but I have to admit I do admire that kind of dedication."

I smiled and got off of his arm to playfully push him.

"Here you go teasing me again," I said, sticking out my tongue jokingly.

"No teasing. Just stating what I noticed. That's it. I promise. I don't want a repeat of earlier."

My stomach at that moment dropped and all the fluttering started again. It was as if there were hundreds of butterflies fluttering around in my stomach and I was helpless to stop them. I didn't know why, but I did like Adrian more than I cared to admit. Even if he was a guy I would normally stay away from, he got under my skin.

I played with my fingers trying to think of a good excuse to make him leave. I needed him to get out of my space so I could think clearly again. He and I wouldn't work. I knew that. I knew that better than he probably did. We were too different from each other and had different goals. It was all I needed to know and for that reason, I didn't want to even think of the what ifs. I could go back to keeping my distance easily. That was the only way I would be able to do that. If he stayed away, I could keep all these confusing feelings at bay.

"Leah?" Adrian said softly interrupting my thoughts and I turned towards him.

"Yes?"

"You are probably the most beautiful girl on this campus. No, you are the most beautiful girl on this campus and you don't even know it," he said.

"What do you mean I don't know it?"

"You're just you. I like you. The real you underneath that mask you wear. And it's beautiful."

And with that, his fingers lightly touched my face to tilt it towards his. I could feel my heart thumping hard again against my chest and all of a sudden I felt lightheaded. He was making me feel crazy, but in a good way. He leaned towards

111

me as my heart raced, and his cologne once again invaded my nostrils. Leaning in, his lips lightly touched mine. Almost grazed them, and I sighed. He took that as a go ahead and his kiss hardened as he pried my mouth open with his tongue. I felt myself tremble as he pulled me into his arms, and my head started to spin. This wasn't supposed to feel this way. I was sure of that. I wasn't supposed to feel dizzy, almost drunk, but at the same time, it felt so good. It felt right. Like I belonged there.

Adrian finally pulled away from me and he looked at me, his expression one of lust and uncertainty on his face.

"I'm sorry. I couldn't help it. Your lips were there and I had to have them again."

"Is that something you do often, just going around kissing girls?"

"I won't lie. I did kiss a lot of girls."

I raised my eyebrow at that. "And now?"

He shrugged. "Now, I only want to kiss you. Make you mine."

"Yours?"

"Yes. Mine!"

"I guess a part of me knew then that you were mine."

"I didn't say that."

"You didn't have to."

"Whatever. And now?"

"I'm telling you so we're on the same page. I don't want anybody else, but you. And I will do whatever it takes for you to understand that. Or for you to let me show you that you are mine."

I was at a loss for words. No one has ever said that before. No one and yet he sounded so sure that he almost convinced me. Almost. I didn't believe him. I wasn't that easy to get with. Maybe I was a personal challenge for him. Maybe he said this to all the girls he came in contact with. The other part of me wanted the rational part of my brain to shut up. What was wrong with a little fun? What could be so wrong about being his? Did I want that?

"I should go. I have to get some rest for practice. Can I see you tomorrow?"

"I don't know if that's a good idea," I said my answer voicing my concerns.

"Please?"

I sighed, feeling backed into a corner. But not wanting to outright admit that I did want to see him again.

"Okay. I'll see you tomorrow."

He smiled then. "Great. See you then." And with that, he touched my face lightly. I closed my eyes, wanting to feel his lips again, and he obliged me. Lightly brushing my lips.

"If we kiss the way we did before, I may want something else. I want something more, but I'm going to try a different approach. I don't want to be that guy with you."

I nodded, both happy and annoyed with that explanation.

Biting his lip, he winked before leaving my dorm room.

I plopped down on the couch again. Were Adrian and I a thing?

My mind raced and I closed my eyes. *What the hell was wrong with me?* How could something that screamed danger feel so good? No matter how much I tried to rationalize

a reason to dismiss what I was feeling, I couldn't. Simply. I

wanted to see him try.

Chapter Nine

Adrian

As promised, I met up with Leah near the field in front of the campus. It was still some light outside. She sat there under a tree, a notebook on her lap and her pen in her hand, writing furiously.

"Hey, there nani," I said to her kneeling to kiss her on the top of her head.

"Hey. How was practice?"

"Brutal. But what else is new? Coach always runs us hard because he wants her to be the best."

"I guess that's good then. Let me just finish up my notes," she said.

I nodded, sitting next to her, watching as she scribbled away in her notebook. She was so concentrated on what she was doing.

"Done. What's the plan?" she asked, putting her things in her book bag.

"I thought it would be nice to go on a date?"

"A date?"

"Yeah. You know when two people decide to go out and get to know each other. And they do different things," I said with a smirk.

"I don't feel like I'm dressed for a date though."

"Don't worry. You look fine."

"But..."

"No buts. You look perfect. You don't need to change. I promise."

"If you say so. I feel so plain right now."

"And?"

"And, if I'm going on a date I should feel more glamorous."

"Don't worry about it. Stop stressing it. I swear you're fine. You are perfect. Okay?" I said, touching her chin.

"Okay," she said, moving her hair behind her ear.

"Oh, and one more thing. You may have to miss class tomorrow."

"Wait, what? You know I can't do that," she exclaimed.

"Have you ever missed a class before?"

"No. Of course not!"

"One day won't kill you. I promise. I want some time with you. You deserve a break."

She glanced at the floor as if she was contemplating what I said.

"And when would we be back?"

"We can get back tomorrow. But I have a few things planned. Is that okay with you? Or are you going to stress over this?" I said half-jokingly.

"Sure. I'll go."

"By the way, you may want to pack a bag."

Two hours later, we arrived in Naples, Florida. Getting out of the car, I went around to open the door.

119

"We're here my lady," I said with a dramatic bow.

"What are we doing?"

"See the boat right there?"

"Yes. What are we doing?" I repeated.

"This boat I rented so we can eat and watch the sunset. And I thought it may be a little more romantic than being in the dorm or near the campus."

Reaching for my hand, I smiled as she took it. We made it to the boat, and she looked around amazed.

"This is a gorgeous boat," she said, squeezing my hand.

Not as gorgeous as you."

I took her to the deck, and we sat down. I went to the fridge that was inside to get the wine and sandwiches that I had sent before we got there.

"So, tell me what got you into football?" she asked, finishing the last bite of her sandwich.

"It was always something I liked to do. As a kid, my mother would have my cousins over and we would play in the backyard. There was something that got the adrenaline pumping even when I was younger. I knew even then that I wanted to be a football player. I had to. And it's like each of us work like a unit almost like a family."

"I get that."

"And you always like writing?"

She smiled, sitting up more in her chair.

"Yes. I did. I would watch stuff going on in my neighborhood and write up mock articles like I was the neighborhood reporter. I always admired a journalist finding the facts or speaking their truth in a way that told a story without hurting anyone. I want to do that. I want to get myself to the point where everyone knows my name," she said.

I nodded, understanding that. I too wanted my name to be known everywhere, but for a different reason.

"I guess we've got more in common than we thought."

"Yeah. I guess we do."

We ate watching the sunset. The wind blowing in her hair. She turned towards me, catching me staring at her.

"What?"

"Nothing," I replied.

"Then why are you staring?"

"Because you're so pretty. Beautiful and all those things."

"Thanks," she said, blushing.

"Thank you!"

We sat there, on the boat looking out at the water and the sky. It was stunning.

"It's kind of chilly now. Want to go inside?" she asked softly.

Looking away, I stared back at the water, trying to ignore the urge to kiss her. To have her right here.

She pulled the shirt over her head, exposing first the small of her back. My dick twitched at that. Pulling it off, I could see the lace bra she wore, holding her breasts in place, her cleavage inviting.

I glanced back at her trying to figure out where she was going.

"Come on, I'm cold. And if we are staying the night on the boat, I want to be on the inside of it."

"Whatever you want," I replied, my voice strained. She grabbed my hand and we walked inside the boat. We kept going until we reached the bed. Sitting down, she patted the space next to her.

"I could sleep in the front you know," I said.

She shook her head. "No. We can sleep in the same bed. Together. Well, eventually..." she said.

I opened my mouth in surprise not sure she meant what I thought she did. But instead of giving me an answer, she replied by pulling me to her. I kissed her then, fervently, my hand grabbing at her breasts.

"I didn't bring you here for this you know," I whispered.

"I know."

"I don't want you to feel like I'm pressuring you."

"You're not. I want you. I wanted you for a while now, I've just been telling myself that I didn't because I didn't want to admit that I liked you."

I laughed.

My tongue ran across her chest, my hands clasping her right breast. I pulled it out of her bra, and greedily put it in my mouth. It was all too much, but not enough. Her skin tasted so good. I licked her nipples, my lips moving down to her stomach.

Sitting up I took my shirt off and my jeans leaving them on the floor.

"You have too many clothes on," I said to her, my voice sounding unrecognizable to me.

"Maybe I wanted you to take them off," she said coyly.

"Oh is that so? I think that can be arranged."

I unbuttoned her pants pulling her sweats off from her body. She wiggled out of her bra, turning it around so she could unclasp it.

I admired her body. She seemed so shy and withdrawn all of a sudden. But she had no idea how amazing she looked. How much I wanted her. How I was sure I never wanted anything as much as I wanted her right then. And I was even surer that I wanted more than a sexual fling with her. But, what if she wasn't ready to take that step with me?

Leah's eyes went to my briefs, a curious expression on her face.

"Do you want to see it?"

She nodded.

Picturing all the ways I could have her, I licked my lips, my mind acting way before my body. Once they both caught up, I pulled out my wallet, grabbed a condom, and placed it on the bed. Pulling down my pants, I stepped out of them and took off my briefs.

I stood in front of her completely nude.

Her eyes roamed my dick. I could see the appreciation in her eyes, and I felt a bit smug. Yes, I had a lot to work with, and I couldn't wait to get it inside of her.

"Are you sure?" I asked, again, knowing that if she said no, it would kill me.

"Yes, I'm sure."

I could feel her wetness through the panties she wore. Leaning over, I took them off, throwing them to the floor. Her slit was wet as I flicked my finger across her clit.

"Damn, you're so wet already. I didn't even do anything yet."

"You didn't have to."

"I think I can do one better though. But, first let me get a taste," I said, opening her legs wider, and leaned into her, my tongue sliding across her clit.

I repeated my previous action. Gasping, her body reacted, her hips moving upwards, her legs tightening around my face.

"You're being impatient," I teased.

"Adrian...you're not being fair."

"You want more," I whispered marveled at the way her body twisted in angles to have more of what I didn't offer just yet.

She barely was able to nod, before my tongue roamed over her bud. She grinded her hips, as I shoved her pussy in my mouth. I licked and sucked on her clit as she moaned, loving the way she sounded. Loving the fact that it was me that she was doing this with. I took one finger and stuck it in, she gasped.

"Oh," she said so softly.

"You like that?"

"Yes."

"Do you want more?"

"Yes."

I slid another finger into her folds and she cried out as I went deep enough that the palm of my hand rested against the lips of her pussy. Pumping in and out, my fingers moving at a slow, but steady pace. She continued bucking her hips against mine, and as she made a yelp and a loud moan, I could feel the muscles in her pussy tighten around my fingers as she came.

Her body shuddered and her eyes were low, lust in them.

She was so demanding. I loved it. Grabbing the condom off of the bed, I rolled it over my dick. Hovering over her. I slide inside of her slowly, and I could see her eyes closed as she tried to relax.

"I swear I won't hurt you. I'll take it slow."

"I know," she whispered.

"Baby, are you ready?"

"Yes," she whispered, and so I entered her and she cried out as my dick found its place. It was home. I was home. She was so tight and so wet that it took everything in me not to become frantic.

My hips moved, and she clamped her hands around my arms, breathing heavy. Lifting her legs, I went deeper and she gasped, biting her lip again.

"You drive me crazy when you do that you know. Biting your lip. Those lips are mine." I nicked them then and she opened her mouth allowing my tongue entrance.

"You're so fucking beautiful. So perfect." My movements were slow and precise. I knew if I sped up it would be over too soon. I couldn't let that happen. I have been daydreaming about being inside her for weeks now.

"Leah, you're killing me right now," I whispered to her, my breath now haggard and heavy.

"So, do something about it," she mumbled.

"Fuck," I muttered and moved with her, her pussy clenching me like a glove, trying everything not to finish before her.

"Ah, baby. Please fuck me," she said, her hands gripped tightly to my arms.

"Are you sure?"

"God, yes. Yes. Please…"

Lifting her legs, I went deeper and she called out, her hips meeting up to meet my strokes. She was so perfect and I groaned out her name as I filled her up, moving in bliss and not wanting this to end, but knowing that it would end and I would have no say so.

"Baby," she moaned, her voice raspy.

"Yes?"

She mumbled something incoherent.

"What do you mean?"

"This is fucking torture. I need to come. I need to come so bad. Please," she begged, her eyes closed.

"Come then. Come for me, baby."

She closed her eyes, as I bit her neck.

"No. Look at me, Leah. I want to see you as you come all over me. I need to see you. All of you. Don't hide from me"

Her eyes opened, and she kept them on me, her mouth, struggling not to make any sound.

"Why are you trying to stop making any sounds?"

"Because I...don't want anyone to hear me," she said breathlessly.

"It's just the two of us on here. You can scream as loud as you want. And if someone does hear, I don't care. I don't fucking care. Let them hear it."

"Adrian!" she screamed out, her body clenching and tightening as she rode the wave of her orgasm.

"It's alright. I got you." I whispered as I slowly slide in and out of her. And even after she had finished, I kept at it moving painfully slow, enjoying how she felt. How her body felt.

"Fuck," I muttered, groaning as I came. I did as she had done for me, looking at her as the pleasure became too much and I kissed her.

"I don't think I've ever had sex like that before," she said.

"Neither have I."

"Really?"

"Yes, really. I know you think that can't be true, but no one has ever made me feel the way you did. I've never experienced that before."

"Same," she whispered. I laid next to her, pulling her in kissing her head and rubbing her back.

I had no idea we would make love, but I had no problem with it either. I couldn't lie though that feeling this way weirded me out a bit. I wasn't used to any girl having me act this way or having me wanting to spend every waking second underneath her or on top of her. But what might have been even worse out of all of this was the fact that I may have already fallen for her.

Chapter Ten

Leah

The next morning, I woke to Adrian kisses on my face. And after another round, I was exhausted and ready to be off this boat.

His finger messed with the edge of my bra, tracing it all the way down to the bottom. I couldn't figure out what his expression was, but he was so focused, that I was mesmerized as he touched my skin gently. He had barely touched me and yet, I was wet. And God did I want him.

And as our bodies entwined with one another it all made sense. You know how when you are taking that ride up the track on a roller coaster? The wind is blowing in your hair, but all you can think about is the anticipation of what's to come. Suddenly, the big drop happens, and it's so sudden. It happens before you get a chance to let go of the anticipation.

That was how it was with him. Slow at first and then all of a sudden. That's how I knew I was in love with him. But I couldn't tell him that yet.

We continued this throughout most of the morning and the afternoon. Him inside of me and me not wanting it to end. It was so strange, yet so familiar. His body on mine, touching me and loving me. We were so wrapped up in each other that we didn't eat a thing.

"We should head back," I whispered in a daze, my head on his.

"If I'm being honest with you, I really don't want to be around anyone else, but you right now. I can't seem to get enough of you," Adrian replied, kissing my neck again.

I shuddered at his touch, moving away a bit.

"As great as this has been, we need to head back. I have to finish homework, and you have to practice don't you?"

"Yes, but…"

"No buts Adrian. And we went through a whole big box of condoms. It's safe to say that we had enough of each other for now."

He twisted his face in a mock pout. "Honestly, I want us to stay here naked, with you. Skin to skin. I can't get enough of you. I don't think I can ever get enough of you."

I smiled but said nothing because I wasn't sure if I could get enough of him either, and as his fingers trailed my skin, heat radiated off of me, and I was tempted to forget that we had responsibilities.

"We have too. Now come and get up my sexy athlete."

"Well, that's the kind of motivation I need."

I laughed. "And somehow I knew you would say that!"

We made it to my apartment building. Adrian held my hand. I could see the stares from other students that lived in the building, trying to figure out what the deal was between the two of us, but I didn't care. I was only concerned with the way Adrian made my body feel. The way he cherished it.

More importantly, could he really handle my heart? It was beautiful and scary at the same time.

"I need to shower and make it to the school library, so I can look up a few things," I told him, but he covered my lips with a kiss.

"Later?"

"Yes," I said.

I took my shower and made my way to the library ready to fact check some history of the school. The anniversary of the school was coming up, and I had to finish the piece. I made my way across the campus. The girl that I saw with Adrian at the bar approached me, a snarky expression on her face.

"Can I help you?" I asked her not really caring if I could or couldn't. For the most part, I wanted to get my work done, and I really didn't care to be reminded of her with Adrian.

"No. I just wanted to give you a bit of a warning," she said snidely.

"About what?"

"Adrian. He's a man whore. He sleeps around and then he gets bored. He always gets bored. It's like his motto or something. You think because you two are fucking now or something that changes things?"

My face flushed because how did she know we slept together, and then I suspected it had to do with everyone watching us when we got back.

"I don't think what Adrian and I do is your concern."

"It is. When he does this kind of thing to all girls."

"I'm not all girls. Nor do I care about anyone else," I said my voice rising. I didn't want to argue with this girl. It reminded me of Adrian groping her at the party. She was pissing me off.

"It's your funeral girlie," she said with a smirk on her face. It took everything in me to not slap her. It was the way she looked at me with her brow raised and that ugly expression on her face. And then I found myself getting mad at Adrian. Mad that he was that athlete who was good looking and had a whole team of girls that knew him intimately the way I did.

"I don't care. I don't care about you or anyone else," I said, walking away trying to keep my heart that was beating wildly in check.

Once I was on the computer I typed furiously, quickly as I angrily put one word after the other. I didn't know why I let her get to me. I questioned whether or not Adrian and I could truly be a thing when there would always be this nagging feeling that there might be someone else. And when he walked into the library, after his practice with a smile on his face, it made my anger worse.

"Hey baby," he said loudly, sitting next to me. The librarian shushed him.

I didn't respond. All the time in the library had let my anger and insecurities fester and I was angry at him though did I really have a good reason.

"Are you okay?" he whispered.

"Yep." It was one word, but filled with so much meaning.

I saved my document, sending it via email to the editor of the paper. I shut the computer down before getting up and walking out of the library, still tight-lipped with Adrian. He followed behind me, his expression one I couldn't read.

"What's wrong with you?" he asked as soon as I made it outside.

I stopped walking and turned towards him.

"How many girls did you sleep with at this college?" I asked.

His expression changed to surprise, he licked his lips a few times.

"Does that matter?"

"When I have your old conquests coming up to me telling me to watch out for you, then yes does matter."

"Who came up to you?"

"That girl from the bar. The one you where your hands were on her breasts." I could see the memory cross his face before he shook his head. His mouth now set in a thin line. He was angry. But then again so was I.

"Really? I didn't sleep with her. Sure, I thought about it, but I didn't sleep with her. I was with you, remember?"

"Yeah, I do. You probably were trying to get into my pants back then."

"But I did get into your pants," he said with a slight shrug.

I narrowed my eyes at him. This wasn't the time for his stupid jokes.

"How many girls did you sleep with here?" I repeated.

"It doesn't matter."

"You probably don't even remember."

"No. I don't. Nor do I care. I'm with you now. I don't give a damn about who I slept with or didn't sleep with. I'm with you now. And only you," he said quietly, but I could hear the anger in his voice.

"So you say!"

"What the hell does that mean?" he shouted.

"I don't know that." And even as I said it, I knew it may have been a stretch, that I had let that girl get in my head.

"I'm going back to my apartment alone. I want to be by myself. Okay?"

Turning away from him and his angry stare, I walked to my apartment. Maybe I overreacted, but he was one of the most sought-after guys from this school. I knew that before. Could I really compete with other girls when he was a guy who had that kind of attention? I wasn't even sure if I wanted to deal with that kind of thing. I needed some time to myself.

I spent the other portion of the night eating ice cream and watching tv. Adrian had called me several times, but I didn't answer him. Hours later, I woke up to someone getting into my bed.

"Marcy, I'm fine," I whispered, not opening my eyes.

"It's me," Adrian said, wrapping his arms around me.

I shifted in the bed so I could face him.

"What are you doing here?"

Marcy let me in. I know you told me to stay away from you, but I can't. I had to see if you were okay."

"I'm fine. I was sleeping."

"I called you all day. Why didn't you answer?"

"Because I didn't want to talk to you. I wanted to be left alone."

I could see that he grimaced, but I didn't care.

"Can I stay and sleep with you?"

"I guess."

"No. Give me an answer. Yes or no."

"Yes," I said not wanting to argue. I closed my eyes again and I could hear nothing but his heartbeat. It was steady, almost comforting.

"I know you were upset with me earlier. That you wanted to know. The reason why I didn't say how many there were because I honestly don't remember. I told you that I was a jerk and I knew what playing football allowed me to do. I had girls after me all the time. But you are different. I want this more than I wanted anything. And I don't want that part of me to affect what we have now."

"Do we really have something now?"

"I would like to say we do. Of course, I don't have all the right answers, but we're together now."

"I'm sorry. All I could think about is what if she was right? What if you did get tired of me and throw me away like I'm nothing to you," I whispered.

He squeezed my body with his arms.

"I will never get tired of you. There is no one else but you," he said.

There was nothing else for me to say at that point. I closed my eyes falling asleep in Adrian's arms, trying my best not to worry that what we had was nothing more than great sex.

Chapter Eleven

Adrian

"Damn it, Robinson! What the fuck is going on with you? You're not focused," my coach yelled out.

And he wasn't wrong. I was still worried about Leah. Even though we spent the night together, she still seemed standoffish and unhappy this morning. I had to get to practice so I didn't get a chance to talk to her the way I wanted to.

"Sorry, coach," I said.

"No sorries here. Whatever is going on you need to let it go, and get your head back into practice If you don't get it together, I will have your ass running laps like no one's business," he said.

I nodded. I spent the next hour doing what he asked. Attacking everything like an animal. I was angry and frustrated and I took it out on my teammates. After practice, coach called me over.

"What's going on with you?" he asked.

"Nothing," I lied.

"I get it. Sometimes you guys get too worried about the girl you're messing with. But this is a big year for you. A big one for Tommy too. You need to stay away from any distractions and keep your head focused on the game. Nothing else."

"Alright coach! I got it," I exclaimed.

"You better, or there will be consequences for your lack of motivation."

As I turned to walk away, coach called me again.

"Adrian, I want you to do 20 laps around the field. It's a reminder on what not to do for our next practice," he said.

I nodded. I knew this was my fault, I wasn't focused enough. And so, I started my laps.

When I finally reached Leah's apartment, I was tired, but eager to see her. I rang the doorbell, realizing the door was open.

"Leah?" I said, walking into the room. "You left the door open." I locked the door and turned around, surprised that her things were thrown on the couch.

Once I reached, her room, I saw Leah sitting on her bed, hunched over. Her eyes were closed, her hands over her face. She seemed in her own world.

"Are you okay, Leah?" I asked, but she said nothing.

"Kuuipo? Talk to me. Tell me what's wrong."

She still didn't answer, so I gently tapped her.

"I feel like I'm dying. I just need a moment," she said, her voice strangled.

"You're worrying me. What the hell is wrong?"

"Panic...attack. It happens sometimes. It'll pass."

I pulled her to me then cradling her on my lap, kissing her face. Her cheeks were flushed, and they felt warm. She didn't look well.

"I think I need to take you to a doctor."

"I'm fine."

"You're shaking, baby. This isn't fine. You aren't fine."

147

Her head turned towards me to look up at me, and she gave me a weak smile.

"Just hold me."

And so I did. Held her in my arms, on her bed that was much too small, rocking her back and forth. She buried her head into my chest breathing heavily. The fear that shot through me was something I had never experienced before. But I didn't let her go. We sat there like that for almost an hour.

"Thank you," she said.

"What was that?"

"A panic attack. Sometimes I have them. And sometimes I don't. Though it seems talking to my mom sometimes trigger them. She just doesn't make sense to me. Like she hates that I'm in college to write. She thinks I need to be doing something else, but I love writing. Is it really that bad that I want a career that I truly love? It seems that most of my conversations with her are about my choices recently, so it's not too much of a surprise that this happened.

148

"I'm sorry. You should do whatever your heart tells you. You had me scared there for a moment."

"Thank you. I appreciate the sentiment. I'm fine. You don't need to say sorry."

"I know, but I don't like that you're unhappy. You seem so strong normally, so to see you like that almost helpless, made me feel worse because I couldn't help you at that moment. I want you to feel better.

She gave me a half smile then. "Thank you. I'm fine. And thanks for holding me."

"Are you sure?"

"Yes. I'll be fine. I promise. I know you need to get ready for your game. I will be there cheering you on. You're going to kill it out there like you always do."

"Maybe you should skip this game."

"No. I'll be there. You won't convince me otherwise."

"Are you always so stubborn?"

"Yes. But so are you."

"We are quite the pair, aren't we?" I said laughing.

"Yep. Go get ready. I'll see you at the game."

Standing up, I placed her on the bed and kissed her. I could do that all day and not get enough of the way her skin felt against mine.

"I don't support that decision at all, but I won't argue with you. I will see you then."

The game was starting and I found myself glancing over to where Leah normally sat with Marcy. I could see her there and she waved at me. My heart swooned. Was that even possible for my heart to swoon? But it did. And here she was at the game. All for me.

When it was my turn to be on the field, I watched as the ball came to me, and as it came. I pass rushed. I was damn good at it. Sacking the other team's quarterback twice. Every time the offense scored, the crowd went crazy, and in turn, I was caught up in the moment. Caught up in the adrenaline from me, my teammates and the school supporting us.

We won the game 28 to 23 and I was so pumped. Tommy and I chanted on the field, the school following suit. I could see Leah from the crowd of faces, and she blew me a kiss I winked and blew one back at her, though I was sure she didn't see it.

Making it to the locker room, the energy was off the chain, and I smiled taking off my jersey. Showering quickly so I can get to Leah.

Grabbing my things, I walked out of the door, I saw my mother standing there with a smile on her face.

"You did good baby boy. I'm proud of you," she said.

I grinned, grabbing her and pulling her tiny body into a hug.

"Thanks, mom. Why didn't you tell me that you were coming today?" I said after I placed her down.

"I wanted to surprise you. And I must say you didn't disappoint. You know there are people watching you right?"

"I know mom. I know."

"Pehea 'oe?"

"I'm good mom. I'm great actually."

"I'm glad to hear it. I want all the things you want baby boy. This is what we have been working for," she said.

And it brought me back to how she was always my biggest supporter when it came to me playing football. My father not so much.

"Where's dad?" I asked anyway.

"You know he is always busy with his hotel. But it doesn't matter. He does it all for us. And you have me. We have each other. The most important thing is ohana. We have each other."

I nodded, saying nothing else on the subject. She always defended him, especially when it came to his preference of ignoring that I loved football. Lived and breathed it. But instead of getting upset, I changed the subject.

"Mom now that you're here, I want you to meet someone who is really special to me."

My mother looked at me really confused as I grabbed her hand and brought her out of the locker room. We walked to the side entrance of the stadium where Tommy, Marcy, and Leah stood waiting for me. I smiled as soon as I saw Leah. It took everything in me not to run over to her and pull her into a hug. Once we reached them. I held my hand out for Leah, which she took.

"Mom, this is my girlfriend Leah. Leah, my mom," I said, smiling at the two ladies in my life.

Leah smiled brightly and reached out her hand to shake my mother's hand. My mother looked at her hand, but didn't take it. Instead, she looked at me.

"What is this?" she asked. I could see Tommy look at me with a knowing look. He knew how my mother could be. I could see the hurt on Leah's face. But she said nothing, as she placed her hand down, looking at me questioningly now seeming uncomfortable.

It's nice to meet you, Mrs. Robinson," Leah said with a small smile, and I appreciated it that she still tried.

"I wish I could say the same, but then again, I would be lying," she said.

Leah faltered and stepped back.

"Adrian, why did you bring me to this girl? This whore will not mess up what we have worked for," she said completely ignoring Leah again as if she was an annoying insect that needed to be squashed and quickly.

Part of me knew where my mother was going with this, but the other half of me knew Leah was like that. I knew my mother wouldn't let me hear the end of it if I said something, besides she was only concerned. And I appreciated that no matter how extreme it was.

I could see Leah's nostrils flare at that, and she looked at me wanting me to say something. Anything. But I didn't.

"Uh, Leah, come on. We'll catch you later," Marcy said pulling Leah. Tommy followed behind them, and I knew that this would be bad. I watched them walk away, before turning back to my mother.

"Ma, why did you have to be so mean? Leah isn't like other girls."

"How do you know that? All college girls are the same. Loose women giving it up to anyone they can. I bet she is only after you because you play football," she retorted with a snort.

"She doesn't even care that I play mom."

"Oh, so she isn't supportive of your dreams?"

"No. That's not what I mean. I meant that her interest has nothing to do with me playing mom."

"I don't trust her. Or women like her," she said, her voice like ice.

"I'm not dad, mom. She isn't like other girls. It's why I like being around her," I said, exasperated.

I was getting aggravated and decided I wanted my mom to leave so I could find Leah.

"Mom, I have to go. The team is going to celebrate the win."

She sighed.

"Fine. But call me tomorrow, we have a lot to discuss."

"Okay, mom." I walked her back to her car and once she drove off, I went to find Leah. I knew everyone was going to the usual hangout so I hoped that she was there.

Once I made my way inside I saw Tommy sitting with Marcy and I saw Leah sitting with them but seeming completely in her own world. Walking up to her, I tapped her shoulder.

"You wanna ditch this and head back?"

"I guess," she said, standing up.

"Marcy are you coming back tonight, or are you staying with Tommy?"

Marcy smiled knowingly and Leah nodded.

"Okay, see you tomorrow. Later Tommy," she said before turning around and walking out of the bar. We made our way to the car, and it was quiet. I knew Leah was upset about what happened with my mother. I was upset as well, but I also knew my mother meant well. I was her only child after all. She had always been super protective of me.

I opened the door to my car so Leah could get in. She did get in without a word and I sighed. This was going to be a long night. I got into the car and pulled off making my way back to her apartment.

"I'm glad that you won your game though. Congrats," she said with a sigh. I knew she was upset. She didn't even look at me when she said it.

"It means a lot to me that you came, Leah."

"Why wouldn't I come? I know how much this all means to you."

"You mean a lot to me as well."

"Okay."

"Just okay?" I said my brow raised.

"I guess."

I groaned. I already knew that from the time I have spent with her, I didn't like it when she said she guessed. It made me feel that she was brushing off whatever was bothering her.

"Baby, I know you're upset. You were upset since after the game. I know my mother can be a handful sometimes and I apologize that she took it out on you. She means well, but she can be abrasive. But I don't want to talk about her. I want to talk about you." I grabbed her hand squeezing it and she shook her head as if she was trying to forget what she wanted to say. But she moved her hand away from me keeping her gaze out the window.

When we reached her apartment, I parked in my usual spot, and then we got out. The quietness was too much and I wanted to say something, anything to lighten the mood, but I also knew that from what I knew about Leah, she would get more annoyed if I said something stupid and so I didn't.

But she didn't walk away. Instead, she turned towards me.

"Are you ashamed of me or something?" she asked quietly.

"Wait? What? No. Of course not."

"So, what was that with your mother? She looked at me like I was the worst kind of person. Did I do something wrong?"

"No, baby. You didn't. You didn't. She's just protective over me."

"I get that, but I did nothing for her to act that way."

"She's my mom. What do you want me to say?"

Leah rolled her eyes. "Nothing, obviously," she said angrily.

"Believe me she isn't as bad as it seems. She's just overprotective of me. My dad...it's complicated."

"That seems code for excuses."

"I swear it isn't. My dad did some horrible shit when they were married, so she always thinks other women do those kinds of things."

Leah crossed her arms. "And what does that have to do with me?"

"Nothing. I'm trying to explain my mother. She wants me to play football and want nothing standing in the way of getting to the NFL."

She laughed, sarcastically. "So, now I'm stopping you from playing football. I thought I was more than that, but what did I know. My mistake."

"No, that's not what I think nor what I meant. She just goes overboard sometimes."

"And that makes me feel better how exactly?"

Sighing, I moved closer to her.

"Leah? Baby, let's not fight okay. I don't want to fight with you. I don't want an argument. I just want to enjoy the rest of my night with you okay?"

"Uh huh," she said sarcastically.

"You think I'm lying?"

"I don't know what to think. I'm just over today."

"Why must you always be this way? Do you like fighting with me?

"You know what, Adrian? I'd rather you left. I want to be alone."

She turned to walk away and I ran after her.

"Leah, please turn around. I didn't mean that baby. I just don't want to fight with you."

"Do I? Do I really? Your mother called me a whore, and you think I want to fight with you. I want *you* to fight for *us*. You wanted this so bad you said, and then you go on this whole tangent about your mom. I get it. She's your mom, but I'm not some random girl you fuck occasionally. Or maybe I am. Maybe that is what this whole stupid thing is. An occasional fuck that lasted much too long."

"Let's talk inside. Everyone doesn't need to know what we're fighting about," I said, noticing the attention we were getting.

"They know everything else right? They probably know every single girl you fucked don't they," she said her voice raised. She started walking towards the building.

I followed behind her trying to keep my anger in check. She was pissing me off. Once we got inside, I followed her to her room.

"Why are you even here? Go back and be your mother's favorite son. You don't need to worry about me now. I'm fine. I don't need this crap. I don't need you."

"She's my mom!"

"So, she gets a free pass to be disrespectful?" she yelled back.

"No. I...You wouldn't understand."

"How wouldn't I? I have a mom too. And yes she loves me and sometimes gets on my nerves, but I wouldn't let her say that about you. I would never let that happen. You can worry about the wellbeing of your child without resorting to insults. It isn't that hard."

"It's not the same thing."

"How isn't it? Yes, you love your parents, but it doesn't mean tolerate things like that either. But of course, I'm the one being difficult right," she yelled pacing again.

"I didn't say that," I yelled at her.

"You didn't have to. My apologies for being the girl you fucked when you wanted to get one off. I guess you're bored of me now, so you send your mom to make it easier on you!"

"Wait? What are you talking about?"

"You know what I'm talking about. Sending her to do your dirty work. I bet this isn't her first time covering for you. You get what you want and then you move on to the next one."

"Stop it."

"And then you play the same game you play with me with some other girl. The same cycle. Girls being too dumb to know the difference. Like me, apparently!"

"Leah—"

"Then you go and sleep with someone else like it's nothing. Like I meant nothing to you. Like I mean nothing to you. It was all about sex, wasn't it? Wasn't it? You stupid, stupid jerk!"

"Damn it, Leah! Stop it. Just fucking stop. Fuck!" I yelled, punching the wall behind her.

She froze then, her eyes wide in fear. She trembled. I calmed down a bit breathing in heavily with a sigh.

"I'm not going to hurt you. I would never put my hands on you. I'm mad. You won't stop. You are saying things that aren't true."

She said nothing.

"You are always so riled up about things. I don't see you that way. I want to be with you. My mom has nothing to do with that."

"If you say so…"

"No! You listen, damn it! Listen. I'm with you because I want to be with you. Nobody can change that. Okay?"

"Maybe I don't want that anymore."

"What does that mean?"

"It means what I said."

"You don't mean that Leah!"

"Yes, the fuck I do! I can't do this. I don't know why I let myself even get involved with you. This isn't me."

"Don't say that," I said half pleadingly closing the space between us.

"I don't owe you a damn thing," she retorted.

"Why are you doing this? Are you trying to intentionally piss me off? It's fucking working."

"Good! Now you know how I feel. How you made me feel by letting that happen. I'm serious though. I don't want to do this anymore."

"You don't mean that," I said, ignoring what she was saying. I moved in closer now, her body so close. I could smell her scent. She was wearing something that smelled like apples. I could feel her anger. But, I was angry too. So angry with her. So angry with myself for still wanting her even after she pushed me away.

Grabbing her face in my hands, I kissed her angrily, feeling too much and, all at once. She opened her lips for me to invade her mouth with my tongue, I groaned. I wanted her so bad. So bad. My hands traveling up and down her spine,

164

and I could feel her body tense up before she relaxed. Picking her up, I held her ass in the palms of my hand and placed on the bed. There was no way I was going to be able to contain myself.

The dress she wore allowed for easy access and I stuck one finger inside of her. She moaned, panting.

"You're so wet, Leah. So wet. This turns you on? Fighting with me turns you on?" I said in half disbelief, but not really caring. She squirmed, and I slid another finger inside of her. She moaned then, but I was angrier than I've been. She tightened around my fingers, she was close, but I wasn't letting her get off just yet.

"I want to taste you. No, I need to taste you. Get my tongue between those lips of yours," I said gruffly.

I darted my tongue over her clit, lapping at her, and biting her. She cried out involuntarily panting, as I took her swollen flesh into my mouth. Tasting her, burying my tongue inside her. She was an addiction. I couldn't get enough of her. The whiny sounds she made seem almost primal, and she shook as an orgasm taking over her. It was a beautiful sight, and my dick twitched as she moaned loudly, her fingers gripping the sheets, trying to crawl away from me. But I held her steady as she moaned.

"You like this? You like me being rough for you? You want me like this? Fighting and pleading with you Leah, baby?"

"Yes. God, yes!" she said. I could see her stomach clench as she moaned again.

I looked at her lips that were now wet and swollen, her mouth partially open and I groaned again. Fuck, she was making this so hard for me. She grabbed my hands and held me down to her as she kissed me again, her body bucked against mine. My dick was so hard that it strained my pants.

I pulled my pants down and slid inside of her. Fucking her slowly at first enjoying every moment of how her body reacted to my touch.

"Adrian," she said again, her voice sounding wounded and I gripped her thighs tighter moving in and out of her.

"Is this my pussy?" I said, my voice not sounding like my own.

"Yes."

"Say it is my pussy. Tell me it is mine."

"It's yours, Adrian."

"Always?"

"Yes. God, yes. Always."

"And you belong to me?"

"Yes. Baby yes. Oh my God!" she screamed out and her body stiffened, her eyes rolling back as she came all over my dick.

But I wasn't done. I grunted, pulling one of her legs, my hips working quicker until I reached my release, waves of pleasure rolling over me. I leaned over her, kissing her stifling the screams that came out of her mouth, as I pumped in and out of her until I couldn't anymore. I was sure if I had her against the wall instead I would've collapsed.

My breaths were heavy, as I slid out of her and moved so I could lie next to her on the bed. It then hit me that I didn't use a condom.

"Baby, we didn't use a condom," I said.

"I know. I…we were caught up," she said, shaking her head. "I'm on the pill though. It should be fine. I hope. And, I'm clean."

"I am too. You're the only women I've slept with unprotected," I said.

There was silence, but both of us breathing heavy. Her body curled into mine. We laid like that for a while before she spoke.

"You know, your mom already doesn't like me and she doesn't even know me. How do I compete with that? How would competing with her even be an option? You think I don't know the routine of mama's boys and what not. I do and I don't want to deal with that. No matter how sexy the son may be. I just don't want to be second to any guy I am with. I would always feel that I would come second to your mother. I can't do that. I just can't."

I chuckled and she rolled her eyes.

"So, this is funny now." She scowled.

"No. Of course not. I like how you get when you are angry it's so sexy. You have no idea how it is for me when I see your face all scrunched up with anger."

"Isn't that how we got into this position?"

"Yeah. But it was good. Fucking great actually."

"It shouldn't have happened."

"Why not?"

"Because I let a moment of pleasure change my mind. It's sex and I let it happen."

"Aloha au ia'oe, Leah. I love you. I don't want to lose you over something like this."

"Pouring it on kind of thick, don't you think?"

"No. I mean it. I care about you. More than I've ever cared about any girl before. I don't know if it's your sass. Maybe it is. But I can't stay away from you. Not even in the slightest. "

"You don't get it. I feel like I need to be with you. It's like I can't breathe if I'm not around you. You consume me. All of me. And I don't know how to handle that. So, when someone says something like your mother said, I don't know how to deal with that either. Especially, when I know what I feel," she said softly.

"It doesn't matter what anyone thinks about us. I don't care if the whole damn world thinks we are wrong for each other. What I do know is how I feel when I am around you. You are the only thing that makes me happy outside of football."

I kissed the top of her head and she sighed into me.

"I don't know."

"You don't have to."

"If you love me like you said you do then you would know that I need to be loved so much that I can't stand it." Her hands trailed against my chest.

"And that's one of the things, I love about you," I said. If you would've asked me this a few months ago, I would've denied it. I would've downplayed the fact that I even liked her. But I knew this was more than that. I loved her.

"I think I love you too," she whispered.

"Really?" I said, happy that she said it back.

"Wait? You think?"

"I don't know if I want to, but I do. I also like your drive. I like how when you play you leave it all on the field."

What else do you like about me?"

"That you are hands down the sexiest guy on this campus."

"And?"

"Ego much?"

"I may never hear this again."

We both laughed.

"And that's even though sometimes you may come off as a guy I wouldn't want around me, I do like being with you."

"You do?"

"I think so. I've never felt any of this before. Even with the sex, it was so much more intense than it should've been. Like we connected on a whole different level."

She was right. I felt that too. The need to be under her, in her and pleasing her until she begged me to stop.

"I love you too, my little sassy minx."

She snorted and sighed. I held her, my massive arms cradling her body to mine. At the moment, nothing else

171

mattered. Not my parents. Not football. Just Leah and me. Together and feeling like with her by my side there was nothing that I couldn't do. Nothing I couldn't beat. The world was our oyster and I was excited about what that would mean for us as a couple. We cemented our feelings by having the best sex I had ever had, even if it was angry sex.

I could feel her body as she relaxed, but I couldn't. My mind was racing. Would she want a life with me out of college and that included football? I didn't have much time to think about it though, because my eyes got heavy and I found myself in the most peaceful sleep I'd had in a long time.

Chapter Twelve

Leah

The contents of my stomach came up once again and I hurled into the toilet, my skin clammy and flushed. This had been going on for almost a month now.

The first time it happened, I was at Adrian's home game and had to leave the stands to get to the bathroom.

"Are you okay?" Marcy asked as I stepped out of the stall.

"I don't know. Ugh, I feel really sick though," I replied.

"Maybe you should go to the doctor." Marcy was worried. She bit her nails whenever she was nervous.

"I'm fine. It is probably a stomach bug."

"I swear if you don't go, I will call your parents," she said threateningly.

"You wouldn't dare!"

"I would because you got me worried. You haven't been eating well either."

"If it gets you to stop with the threats, I will go. After my next class."

"Good," she replied with a half-smile.

But even as I made that agreement, there was the part of me that suspected what it might be. I didn't know how because I took my pill every day. But just as I was about to get ready for my class, I had to rush to the toilet all over again. The stomach acid made me feel worse, as I threw up everything that I had already tried to eat. It was then that it confirmed my suspicions.

"I'm bringing you a test. You lay down and relax," Marcy said, rubbing my back. I cleaned my face and sighed. She walked me back to our dorm room, and I laid on my bed.

"Don't do anything crazy. Just relax. I will be back with some ginger ale and a pregnancy test," she said.

I barely could nod, but I pulled the covers over my head, closing my eyes.

What seemed like hours later, but in reality was about an hour, Marcy came back in with a bag full of stuff. She sat on the bed next to me. I was half asleep, but I knew it was her.

"How are you feeling?"

"I don't know," I said with a half sob. I was also extremely moody. Moodier than my norm.

"You want to take the test now?"

"Aren't you supposed to wait until morning as that is usually more accurate that way?"

"We could. However, in light of the way you have been feeling, I don't think we can wait until morning. Besides, it's better we know now rather than later," she said sounding like my mother.

"Fine. I will take it now. If it gets you off my back," I said sharply. "I'm sorry. I'm on edge."

"It's fine prego."

"Ha ha," I said, rolling my eyes and going to the bathroom. Marcy grabbed the test following behind me. Once inside, I opened up the box and read the instructions. *Pee on the stick, wait 3 minutes. Not too hard.* So I did what was asked and Marcy set her watch to wait for three minutes. It was the longest three minutes of my life.

Once her watch started beeping, I looked down at the test, my nerves on edge. When I saw the results, my heart plummeted into my stomach and I started trembling with so many emotions passing over me. There on the stick were two pink lines. Not the one line that I was hoping for, but two. I was terrified. I was on the pill. I took it religiously. But here it was slapping me in the face, that the pill might not have meant a damn thing. And what was I going to do with a baby and how would Adrian take this. I tried to think of all ways this could've happened, and then it hit me. The day after I was with him on the boat, I took my new pack of pills a day later than normal. Shit!

"Wow. Congrats?" Marcy said not sure of what my response was.

"What am I going to do?" I said absent-mindedly.

"Look at it like it's a blessing. I know the timing kind of sucks, but this doesn't mean your life is over. It could be just beginning," Marcy said.

"You sound like some kind of motivational speaker," I replied.

"But you love me. And I'm right."

"I'll let you have that. I think one of my biggest worries, is that I don't know how to tell Adrian."

"Just tell him the truth. I think he'll be okay with this, but if he isn't I will kick his ass. I don't care how big he is."

We both laughed at that.

"For now let me just get okay enough to make it to the game. I can deal with Adrian later."

But he has his whole life ahead of him. What if football is more important? What if he wants to break up now?

Marcy nodded, grabbing my hand. I threw the test in the garbage. I couldn't walk around with that on me all day. This was the second to last game before the Peach Bowl. The Vipers record was 8 to 2. I was sure they would win this one, and hopefully, Adrian being in a good mood would change the worry I was feeling.

But I couldn't focus. My mind was on the fact that I would be a mom. For most of the game, I zoned out. My thoughts were all over the place. I could see Marcy stand up, as the crowd around me let out a collective gasp, and I looked up to see someone running onto the field. I stood up trying to see what had happened.

"I think someone's hurt," I heard someone say from behind me. I stood up then, trying to see who it was, looking around the field to see Adrian's jersey. I couldn't see it. It was then that I saw Tommy hovering over the field, that I realized who it was. It was Adrian. The team surrounded him, but I needed to get to him. I needed to be by his side. Moving off the bleachers, I made my way down running onto the field. I didn't care that I could potentially be stopped, I had to make sure he was okay. Other staff members of the team tried to stop me until Tommy spoke.

"Let her go. He would want her there," he said.

I looked at him and mouthed thank you before I reached Adrian, who was now on the stretcher screaming in pain. My heart felt like it was outside of my chest. Maybe it was just a sprain. But as I heard his wails of pain, I knew it was something more serious. Squeezing his hand, I followed as they carted him off the field. I didn't care about the game anymore. I wanted to be by his side, even if it meant this was the end of our relationship.

They took him into the locker room as the team huddled over him saying things here and there. I only heard bits and pieces of the conversation. My stomach twisted in knots as I waited to hear what would happen. It seemed like hours. But Tommy finally came to me.

"He most likely has to get surgery. He is getting an MRI, but they seem to think it is an ACL tear?"

"Is that bad?" I asked.

"Yes. It can be. He will have surgery and physical therapy. The biggest concern is if he will be the same player after he rehabs and gets better," Tommy replied.

I let out a sob. One that didn't sound like me. Of all the things that could've happened today, this wasn't the thing I expected. This was terrible. I knew Adrian well enough to know that he would be devastated about this. After some thought, I decided I would tell him after surgery. I needed to at least get it out there. If he didn't like it then, that was something I would have to accept, but he needed to know.

One Week Later

Some hours after his surgery, I watched him sleep. I held his hand, talking to him.

"You know I didn't think I would be in this position. I never wanted to feel this way about someone, and yet even though we haven't been together long enough, I feel that we were brought together for a reason. I know you're strong and you'll get through this. We will get through this. Together. You and me. And I need you here. I need you to be here for me and our baby. I don't know what I'm doing yet, but I want to decide with you or discuss with you. I know neither one of us are ready, but we can do this. I know we can," I said, wiping the tears from my eyes.

"You're pregnant?" I heard a woman say, and I turned around to see Adrian's mother standing there.

"Yes. I'm pregnant. I found out the day Adrian got hurt. I didn't get a chance to tell him yet," I said my throat feeling like a frog inhabited it.

"Is it his?"

"Of course it is. I haven't been with anyone else."

"Hmm. I find that hard to believe. You think you can trap my son with a baby. You think he would give up his career for you and some bastard child," she said coldly, her voice calm. So calm in fact that I wasn't sure if I heard that correct.

I shook my head. "No. I don't want him to give up his career. I want him to know that's all," I said, trying to keep my voice from wavering. It was definitely hormones because my normal response wouldn't have been to cry.

"You should get rid of it. I'll give you the money for it," she said nonchalantly.

"No! Why would I? This isn't a decision you get to make. Sorry," I replied sarcastically.

"Get out. And leave my son alone, you bitch! You will not ruin his life. I will make sure of it," she said.

"He wants me here."

"If you don't leave, I will have security drag you out."

I thought about the alternatives to get into it with his mother here and decided I would talk to him once he was discharged. I didn't want to make his recovery any worse than it needed to be. I was after all, just his girlfriend. Not his wife. Not his parents. And I understood that, but it didn't make me feel any better, that he was here and his mother took me as a threat when all I wanted to be here until he woke up.

I decided to walk around a bit. I knew Marcy would be waiting, but I needed some time to think. I was emotional and the tears came falling again. *My parents didn't even know that I was pregnant and I knew they too would think I was giving up my life for a guy I didn't know that well. Maybe his mother is right. Maybe I need to get rid of this baby. Or keep it and just go on with my life. He can have his life.*

This continued for 3 days. I would try to see Adrian, and his mother would make sure I couldn't get to his room. I was sure that he wondered where I was, but I had no way of reaching him when his mother stood guard like a watchdog.

On the third day, I took my time getting home. I was distraught. I window shopped a little, just trying to get my mind off of the current status of my life. How could I possibly have a child right now? There was also the fact that I would have to try and be there for Adrian, who I knew was going through tons of emotion right now. After it seemed that I cried so much, I couldn't cry anymore, I started to head back home. I didn't have my car, and I didn't feel like calling a cab. I wanted to delay the inevitable question of what I was going to do. I also had to tell my parents as well.

"I'm sorry," I said, bumping into a tall man. He nodded before crossing the street. I glanced at him as he talked to some guy and turned back around.

Funny, that was the same way I met Adrian for the first time.

I could sense that I was being followed, and I turned around. Two guys walked behind me. While people walking wasn't out of the norm, it was out of the norm to stare at me the way they were staring at me. It was a bit unnerving. Every time I turned back around, they were staring, keep the same distance behind me. I knew I was being followed, but why? I didn't have anything.

I turned down a different block out of my norm, and they followed. I went and walked into a store to get something to drink. I thought I had lost them until I saw them behind me again. The same two guys from before.

I kept walking, hoping that I would run into someone I knew, not realizing that there wasn't anyone outside but me and them. My pace turned into a jog. Once it seemed I got some distance, I slowed down thinking maybe I can hide somewhere until I was sure they were gone. I was grabbed from behind. The man's arms were strong, and I struggled.

"Please, you don't have to do this," I whimpered.

"Shut up!" the other one said, making his way to me and the guy that held me.

"Give me your wallet," he said. Trembling, I opened my bag ready to give them the wallet, and as I put my hand into my bag, I decided to see if I could escape.

Pulling my hand back out, I slapped the guy in front of me. Hard, but not hard enough. He sneered at me, slapping me back harder. My lip split and I could taste the metallic of my blood as it touched my tongue. Giving the wallet, I held my hands up. Hoping that was all they wanted.

"I swear I won't say a word," I whispered, shaking where I stood.

"Of course you won't!" he said, his mouth spreading into an evil grin. He punched me hard then, knocking me into the ground. He grabbed, my shirt and I tried to take another swing He caught my fist, pressing his arm against my throat. The guy behind me, let me go and I fell to the floor. I cried out as the guys kicked me in the stomach. It was pain and dizziness. Too much pain for me to call out the way I wanted.

I wanted to scream not the baby, but for some reason, I couldn't say the words out.

"Anthony, will be happy and we can get paid," I heard one of them say and I was trying to process that. *Anthony? It couldn't be.* My vision blurred and all I could remember is a sick grin, as his boot hit my stomach one more time.

When I did wake up, I had an IV and a mask over my face. My throat was dry, and I felt like shit. Marcy sat there, her eyes red from crying. She looked over at me, letting out a sob. She sat up grabbing my hand, her eyes relieved.

"Oh my god. Leah, I was so worried about you. I thought I lost you. You were lying there not moving, helpless. I don't know what I would've done without you," she cried kissing my forehead. "I'm glad you are up."

I was tired, and could barely move. My body felt like a train had hit it.

"Don't talk. I'm going to get the doctor," Marcy said, as she rushed out of the room.

Moments later Marcy came in followed by the doctor came in afterward, his face like stone.

186

"Ms. Hunter I am glad you're awake. You should recover nicely, but did you know you were pregnant?"

I nodded.

Wait? Were? What did that mean?

"I'm sorry to tell you, but you lost the baby," he said. The bed shook with my cries, as Marcy wrapped her arms around me crying along with me. Sure, I didn't have it all sorted yet. It was all still a big shock. But, even so, it didn't it didn't mean it hurt any less. It hurt all that much more.

Chapter Thirteen

Adrian

I sat in the doctor's office two months after surgery. I was

sore, and in pain most of the time, but they needed to check in

on me again, so here I was. They said I was recovering nicely,

but all I could think about was how my football career was

potential over before it even began.

I had asked my mother countless times did she hear

from Leah, but she kept insisting that she didn't. It was odd

that Leah wasn't there when I woke up. As if as soon as I got

hurt, she went MIA. Mom had moved me back home so I

could get better, but that didn't excuse Leah from not even

being at the hospital. Maybe my mother was right after all.

Leah didn't care for me. How could she if she hasn't been

around while I tried to recover from one of the worst things

that had ever happened to me.

There was a knock on the door, and Leah walked in, her hair in a bun. She looked different. Tired, like she hadn't slept in a long time. There was another emotion on her face, which I couldn't place. Her face was slightly bruised. And something else that was on her face, an emotion I couldn't place, her face slightly bruised.

"Hey! How are you feeling?" she said softly walking over to me.

A part of me was angry with her. Angry that she seemed so calm. She didn't care about my wellbeing this whole time.

"Where have you been?" I asked her instead.

"When?"

"This whole time?"

"Oh. Most recently, I was in the hospital," she said.

My eyes softened at that.

"Another panic attack?"

"No. I wish it was as simple as that. I would've preferred it. Though I'm surprised I didn't have one yet. How are you feeling?"

"As good as one can feel in this situation. It sucks that I have to be on crutches. It sucks that I have to learn to do the things I did already with no problem. The things that were natural. And then the doctors think I should stay away from football until I get better."

She sighed softly, sitting in the chair that was next to me.

"I found out you were here today because of Tommy. Your mother has been making this quite difficult. Well, to see you I mean. I have been trying to see you even before I was in the hospital. Your mom made sure I couldn't come to your room. There are so many things I want to tell you. So, many things that I don't know how to tell you," she said.

"You can tell me."

At that moment, my mother walked in, her eyes narrowed once she saw Leah sitting down next to me.

"What is she doing here?" she asked me.

"Checking in on me. Obviously," I replied.

"I wanted to see if he was okay. I have to talk to him anyway," she said, but my mother ignored her. The lines around her eyes were tense, almost as if she was near popping a blood vessel.

"Oh, she has something to tell you huh? Trying to spin this in a way that doesn't sound too bad?"

"What? No. I have to tell him what I was trying to tell him the day you kicked me out of the room. What I have been trying to do, but you made sure I couldn't," Leah said her voice raised.

"I told you to leave because I didn't want you to break my son's heart."

"That's bullshit," Leah said.

I looked between the both of them. *Break my heart. What the hell was going on?*

"What are you talking about mom?"

"Leah has been cheating on you. It was why I kicked her out. I spoke to the young man whom she cheated with. It wasn't worth getting you upset, especially right after surgery. But, now you know."

"That's a lie!" Leah screamed.

But as the two of them went back and forth, all I could think about was first I get injured during an important game, tear an ACL, have to have surgery, and now Leah cheats on me. After all she'd said about me and other women. Maybe, my mother misunderstood, but my mother has always wanted the best for me. It made no sense for her to lie to me.

"Is this true?" I asked, stopping them both.

"No! I didn't cheat on you. It had nothing to do with that. I do need to talk to you, but I rather talk to you in private."

"Of course she does. So, she can fool you again, and make you believe she is an honest woman. She doesn't love you, son," my mother said.

I thought about what she said and I got angry. I knew I was taking out my issues on Leah. I knew it, but I didn't want to hear anything else. Especially, when I was already dealing with this injury.

"Leah, I need you to leave," I said so softly that at first I wasn't sure if I said it out loud.

"Excuse me?"

"Leave! Just get out of here!"

"Why? You believe her?"

"Why would my mom lie to me?"

Leah laughed bitterly, hurt in her tone.

"You got to be kidding me! I don't get how you don't see what's going on here. It is right there in your face. Your mother treats you like you're her husband. It's weird. No mother should be this hard on about her son. She treats you like you two are fucking or something," she said.

"How dare you?" my mother said, but Leah wasn't done, as she raised her hand.

"I wanted to see you. She told me I couldn't. I had to deal with my own shit and still I worried about if you were okay. If you were alright. What would the next step be for you? For us? Did you miss me? Because I missed the fuck out of you, and yet you still ask me to go like I mean nothing?"

And as she said this I couldn't shake what my mother had said. She missed me, but was with some other guy? I also was still angry about the fact that I got injured. Angry that my dad almost seemed happy that I did. I wouldn't drag her down this hole with me, and if my mother was right about her cheating, she had already moved on. It would be for the best.

"I don't want to do this anymore. We are done," I said sharply. I could see the conflicting emotions on Leah's face. She tilted her head, eyes wide, her breathing heavy. And then a cloud of fury came over her.

"I can't believe you. You believe her. I understand she's your mom, she wanted nothing to do with us being together. Don't you see that?" she yelled.

My mother at that moment walked out of the room, though I wasn't sure why.

But I couldn't stop myself, I was angry, and so I lashed out at her. Took it out on her, the person I loved. There was no way, she would be happy with me. Not with me feeling the way I was. And not with the fact that my mother hasn't steered me wrong. She seemed to know many things that I didn't. I was sure it was the same now. I had to let her go, and the only way to do that was to hurt her.

"I don't love you, Leah. I lied. I said what I could so you will sleep with me. It's a game that I won too. You ate it

195

up. I told you I don't do this kind of thing. And yet, you still thought it'll be different. Thought you could change me? You wanted me to be this perfect guy for you. A guy who didn't say stupid shit and get with whatever woman I wanted so bad, but I got news for you, he doesn't exist! He never existed. He never will," I said coldly.

Leah started to laugh. A laugh that sounded almost manic, but then she stood up, her hands balled into fists. She kicked the chair, before giving a heavy sigh, and that was when she looked at me. Her face wounded.

"You know what Adrian? You're right. I did eat it up. I let the fact that you somewhat got a rise out of me mean something. I let the fact that I loved you being inside of me cloud my judgment. I regret this whole fucking thing. I regret being with you. You're not worth this. I knew this all along and I told myself I was making too much of it. I was being too hard on you. I had to relax. I wished I would've listened. But it doesn't matter now. You're not worth this kind of pain. You're not worth me crying or feeling anything. But you know what? I will do all the things I said I would. And you will still be a mama's boy. Eventually, it won't bother me anymore. You won't mean a thing. You'll have to live with the fact that you messed up something good. I hope this bothers you every single day for the rest of your fucking life. I hope you get all you fucking deserve, you piece of shit."

And as I watched her body shake in anger, tears falling down her face, I wanted to get up and hobble over to her, but I didn't.

"Ma'am, I'm going to need you to leave," the guard said reaching to grab her. My mother stood there behind him, a smirk on her face.

Leah looked over at him, her gaze filled with fury.

"Don't touch me. I'm leaving," she said, walking out of the door. And as my mom talked to the other guard, I felt a little piece of my heart break as I watched the love of my life walk out of it. And I did nothing to stop it.

Chapter Fourteen

Adrian

NYC (2016)

I sat in the meeting room waiting for Leah to come from her

office. I had only been here for about five minutes, but I

already liked the way the staff was attentive and friendly with

one another. I had my business phone in my hand scrolling

through the latest emails. As usual, there were many and a few

missed calls from my father. It wasn't like he didn't call my

personal phone already. But I was sure most of the problem

had to do with the fact that he couldn't reach me. According to

him, I was supposed to always be accessible.

Moments later, Leah knocked on the door and stepped

into the room. I took in her black pencil skirt and white blouse

that showed her ample breasts. While the blouse wasn't too

tight, it was tight enough that I can see the cleavage and I wondered if they still felt the way they did before in my hands. She didn't look like she aged a bit.

"Good morning. Sorry to keep you waiting, Adrian. I had to take a call. You can follow me to my office."

"Morning. Sure," I said, getting up and following her out of the room.

I made my way past the cubicles of reporters until I could see a long hallway that had magazine titles across the wall. Some of them I recognized from the past stalking I did with Leah's work. I watched the sway of her ass as she walked and it took everything in me not to grab it. But we were at her job and it was good to be professional. Besides, I didn't want to risk her slapping me like she did all those years ago.

"Here we are," she said opening up a sliding door.

"Ladies first." I held the door open so she could walk in first and closed it behind me.

Her office was pristine. It was professional and stylish. She had awards lining up on the walls. And some plants here and there. I saw two photos on her desk. One with her and Marcy, her friend from college. She looked the same. She was the reason I met Leah in the first place. Rather the reason Leah was at the game that day. The other was one that showed Leah smiling and seemingly carefree. Now, she looked so tense. Maybe it was because of me. There was also a desk plate that said her name and underneath it said Senior Editor and Head Writer. It explained the office. She had another one more so on the right of her desk and it said "Sassy, Classy and A bit Smart Assy" and I loved it as it reminded me of her. She was all those things and more. So much more. And I wondered if she added to those things that were more.

"You can have a seat over there. Again, I apologize for the wait. Sadly, it never is much downtime here."

"It's okay. It's fine. I was there maybe ten minutes. Nothing too bad."

"My boss wanted me to meet you here. There is a location that I normally would go for interviews, but for some reason, she thought we should go together to try to avoid any press since most people do know who you are now. Is that okay?"

"Yep. Perfect."

"Let's head to the car. I have a driver waiting downstairs. I don't want to keep you," she said in her business-like tone.

I wanted to tell her that she didn't need to rush on my behalf because I had cleared the whole day for this interview. So, I could see her, but I kept my mouth shut. Something told me that I made her uncomfortable.

I followed her back out of her office down the hallway until we reached a lone elevator. This elevator will take us to the back, where the car is waiting. We got in the elevator standing on opposite sides. I would have preferred if she was next to me, but I was okay because I got to look at her as she stared at the floor.

You would think it wouldn't be possible for someone to get more beautiful with time, but she was. She was gorgeous in her element. Even when she stayed as far away from me as the elevator walls would allow.

The door opened, and she walked out first heading to the door, pushing it open, the car sat there with a driver waiting outside.

"Good morning, Ms. Hunter," the driver said.

"Good morning, George. Sorry, for the early appointment."

"It's my job."

"George this is hotel owner, Adrian Robinson. Adrian one of the company's drivers, George."

I was surprised she introduced him as if she was a friend, but I held my hand out.

"Nice to meet you, George."

"Nice to meet you too Mr. Robinson. A pleasure."

George opened the door, and Leah got in first with me following right behind her. The ride over was quiet. She scrolled on her phone, and I knew it was because she was trying to avoid any other conversation. The old me would've questioned it, but I didn't. I let her have her silence. I would change that after this interview.

Once we reached the restaurant, we were taken to the rooftop. There was a table with a nice breakfast spread.

"This is nice," I said, breaking the long silence.

"Yeah. This place always gives us the best during the magazine's interviews. You want anything?"

"Just a bottle of water."

"You're sure?"

"Yes, Ma'am."

Nodding, she went over and made a coffee, and grabbed a bottle of water. I decided I could get the bottle of water myself and walked up behind her.

"I can get my own water, you know," I said, but she jumped seemingly startled that I was that close to her.

"I wasn't expecting you to be right behind me," she said with a small wave.

"I thought I'd help and get my own water since you're making a cup of hot coffee."

She nodded and turned back around. I took that as my cue to head back to the table. I sat down waiting for her. I watched her as she sat across from me placing the coffee on the table. She tucked a bit of her hair behind her ear.

"I have some of the things you said on our lunch date, written down as reminder notes. I will ask you some questions and you will answer them. There will be some inclusion about your history before hotels. The reasons you felt NYC was the right place for another hotel, and some other stuff for the background piece. I will get it all pretty and it will go to press for the next issue."

"Straight to business, huh?" I said with a chuckle.

"Is there really anything else that needs to be talked about at this moment?" she said rather bluntly and I smiled at that.

Leah was always blunt, to the point, and rarely did she mince her words. She was a firecracker. A hell raiser, if you will, and I loved all of it. Loved it all. It was really one of the things that attracted me to her outside of looks. While she thought she was a nerd, I thought she was fire and air. Air I wanted to breathe in. She was beautiful.

"Still the same Leah."

"Not really." It was said softly. So softly that I wasn't sure if I heard it all.

"Okay. Let's get started. I will be asking you questions, taking notes and this right here is my recorder and I

204

only use it to make sure I get your words 100 percent correct," she said pointing to the small recorder on the desk.

"You're the boss, Leah," I said with a smile.

"How does it feel knowing that women across the world find you to be one of the most eligible bachelors?"

"I was surprised. I didn't know this kind of thing still happened. Seemed more like all the hoopla over the guys that were celebrities when I was a teen. I saw the other competition and I must say the fact that I was chosen to be the top fifteen is crazy."

"Where were you born?"

"Florida. Pensacola to be exact. But you know that though."

"Yes, I do. But just running down the basics if that's okay?" she said tapping her pen.

I shrugged. "That's fine by me."

"Okay, and where do you reside now?"

"I lived in many places. Florida, Vegas, California, but I will be residing in New York City very soon."

"And what is it that you do?"

"I run hotels. My goal is to make every guest's stay comfortable, and enjoyable. Make sure they get their money's worth. My dad was the man behind the dream and I am more so keeping the train going. I will have the most control over the New York one."

Leah nodded writing it down. I was sure she knew that already, but I watched as she jotted down her notes, her face fixed in concentration.

"Best pick up line?"

I laughed. That was a switch.

"Uh, I don't think I have one. At least not anymore."

Leah looked up at me to raise a brow, an amused expression on her face, but she didn't say anything.

"And what would it take to get your attention from a woman?"

"A connection. Before I was a bit shallow, I know that. I was the guy who only thought about the way a woman looked first. If she had big breasts or a big ass I was into it. It took me some time to appreciate that there's more to women than their looks. Now, I rather some kind of a connection first.

Spark something inside of me. Make me want to be around you. All the other things like quirks, compassion, honesty, intelligence and empathy all play a role after that."

She paused, an expression I couldn't read on her face. Slightly shaking her head, she continued.

"Are you saying you didn't appreciate those things before?"

"Yes and no. Again, I was a shallow guy. But I always like an honest and quirky person. Those kinds of the people are the most fun."

"What do you do when you're not working?"

"Am I ever not working?"

She smiled a bit. "I understand that."

"I work out a lot. Probably more than most people. Spend time with my mom when I can."

Leah winced a bit. And her face flushed. She stopped writing for a moment, and sighed.

"Are you okay?" I asked her concerned. I wasn't sure why she reacted that way, but she gave a forced smile.

"I'm fine. Thanks. I'm sorry, you were saying?" she said changing the subject.

I paused again, but decided not to ask.

"I attend functions here and there. And of course watch football."

"Is that different now? Watching football when you played in college?"

"Yes and no. A part of me always wonder the what ifs. If this was younger me, I would say it bothered me that I wasn't out there on the field, giving it my all. After my injury, I wasn't the same player. And I know some people bounce back from ACL injuries, but I wasn't one of them. Now, I see it as a past time to enjoy. Watch those who did make it like Tommy."

"Hold on, just making a note to add who Tommy is when I type all of this up."

I took a sip of my water.

"And what is something that you would like to tell everyone that isn't known?"

"If I could go to bed by 10 pm every single day I would."

"Really?"

"Really. Call it getting older, but some days I'm so tired. I don't know how I keep going."

"A good cup of joe," Leah said with a smile, putting her pen down to take a sip from the coffee cup that sat in front of her.

"Yes, sometimes."

She reached out to grab some notes that were fluttering in the wind, and in doing, so she knocked down my phone from the table.

"I'm sorry. I didn't mean to knock your phone down," she said, her expression one of worry, her head creased from frowning.

"It's fine."

She bent over to pick it up. "I hope it isn't damaged." She looked it over.

"Here's your phone" She handed it over to me. Her fingers brushed mine and I could feel a current go between the two of us. It was almost electric.

She froze and sat further back in her chair sat back down, picking up the pen. She began to tap it against her notepad. I knew it was because she felt what I did. It was still there. I was sure of it.

"Are you ready?"

I nodded.

"Best trait?"

"I think I can be a bit unrealistic sometimes. More so in a good way. Like I'm sure I can make anything happen if I put my mind to it."

"And worst trait?"

"Sometimes I'm much too hard on mistakes I made. I'm learning to work on that."

"Aren't we all? What is the most romantic thing you have done before?"

"If we're being honest. Not much. It's not that I don't want to be romantic. It's just that I haven't had a chance to."

"And do you have the chance now?" She stared at me then, her big brown eyes looking at me curious to what I was said, her mouth partially open as she used to do all the time when she had many things that she wanted to say.

Ah, so maybe she was interested.

"Maybe. I'm just not too sure if the woman I want is interested in anything more with me."

"I'm sure any woman would be happy to have you, bachelor," she said a bit sarcastically.

"But I don't want any woman. I want one woman specifically."

"Why is that?" she said, her eyes telling me I was on thin ice.

I shrugged. "Let's just say I believe in second chances and I hope she does too."

She put her pen down again. Turning the recorder off, and closed her eyes sighing.

"Why are you doing this?" she asked.

"Doing what?"

"You know what. I don't think I need to spell it out."

"I'm being honest."

I could see the wheels turning in her head.

"Maybe not that honest."

"Why not? If we are doing a piece which requires you to ask me questions, then I should be as honest as possible, then why wouldn't I be that honest?"

"Because this deals with me. I know where you were going. And I don't think it would take anyone else too long to figure that out either."

"Maybe. Maybe not. I'm not going to lie though. It is what it is. It is what I feel. It is the truth. I didn't say anything purposely to make you uncomfortable."

"I know," she replied softly. "I know. This is just too close to home. I shouldn't have agreed to do this. It's too personal for me."

"I know. And I swear it isn't on purpose," I said, putting my hand over hers.

She froze her eyes searching mine, and then she shook her head. I removed my hand, wanting to keep it there, but trying to respect her space.

"I'm sorry. You're right. Let's finish this."

After taking a sip of her coffee, she turned the recorder back on.

"Okay, what's your idea of the perfect date?

I folded my hands together mainly so I wouldn't touch her hand again.

"I think it depends. It could be a romantic candlelight dinner. Making love in front of the fireplace. Cooking for that special someone completely naked. Or even something as regular as driving bumper cars. It depends on the woman."

"I actually like that answer. I'm sure our readers will too."

"One thing everyone knows about you."

"I played football as an outside linebacker in college."

"One thing that everyone wouldn't know."

"I sometimes watch rom coms and romance movies, but there is a story behind that."

I gave her a wink and she gave me a look if surprise, before chuckling.

If someone was to ask you what ethnicity do you identify with what would you say?"

"I'm a **hapa haole**. I'm of mixed race. My mother is of native Hawaiian descent and my dad of Irish descent. While I believe I hold both sides dear to me, I am really close to my Hawaiian side, just as much as I am to my mother."

"Any tats?"

"Just one. On my back. It is pretty big."

I pointed towards my back as if she could see it through my shirt.

"Is there a reason for just one?"

"Yes and no. It's a back tattoo with many meanings. Things that are important to me."

"How long did that take?"

"Many sessions. Way too many sessions."

She laughed genuinely.

"What's the best way to say I love you?"

"Hmm. That's a good one. Letting her keep the hoodie she said she would borrow, but never gives back."

Leah looked at me and raised an eyebrow. It was something that she did before. She started laughing again.

"That's a good one," she said, grinning, and shaking her head as she wrote.

"Seriously though, I think letting the words causally come out is the best way. I think it's more honest that way. Or whatever way she would know that I meant every word."

"What was your resolution for this year?"

"To stop being so agitated at things that aren't in my control."

"Good one."

"Any social media?"

"Nope. Though I should probably get some."

"Any advice to our readers?"

"Uh. Be you! Do what makes you happy. Go after all the things you want no matter how hard it may be to obtain them," I replied.

"Great advice. It was awesome having you with us."

Leah clicked off the recorder and put her pen down.

"That wasn't too bad was it?" she asked.

"No. Not at all. Thank you for doing this."

"No problem. Actually, thank you. While there were other bachelors, you're the only one who is getting a real spotlight on this for this magazine. We asked a few questions here and there about the other bachelors, but it was more for the piece as a whole. Well, my colleagues did. But for you, my boss wanted to pull out the stops since you would be in New York, and you got this hotel opening up so it ties you closer to the city. We will be following you to some of your hotel stuff and taking a photo shoot separate from the one all of you bachelors take."

"Sounds good."

Leah sat back in her chair, her hands lightly tapping the table. And while she seemed to be a bit nervous, she still looked like the queen bee and I would do anything to get a taste of her honey again.

"I will type all of this up and get it all ready for publication. I guess we should set up something with the photographer. What is your availability for this upcoming week?"

I took my phone out, looking at my schedule. "I have some free time during Tuesday if that is good for you."

"We can set it up. It works for me," she said.

I watched as she marked it down.

"What are your plans for the rest of the day?" I asked her.

"Uh, I have to start typing these notes and answers from this up, and then handle some other things."

"Are you free for dinner?"

"Well, I...uh. I don't know if that is a good idea."

"As friends only."

"I still think it would be best if the both of us keep it professional. I don't want anyone to get the wrong idea."

"Is that a bad thing?"

"Well, yeah. You are an eligible bachelor. Can't be caught being attached right? Wouldn't that be bad for the admirers?"

"You and I know that neither one of us cares too much about that."

"You and I also both know why it isn't a good idea," she said, her voice raised a little higher than before.

"Maybe I do. But if you're telling me you still don't feel something between the two of us, then I would say that you're lying. It seems easier now doesn't it? Not all the drama and pain we caused each other."

"Each other?"

"You don't think you caused me any pain?"

"No, I don't. And if I did, you definitely caused me more pain than I caused you," she said rolling her eyes. She stood then, putting her things angrily in her bag. Yes, I knew we broke up on bad terms, but the way she looked at me told me it still bothered her just as much as it did when it all went to shit.

"You have no freaking idea. None. You come back into my life because the universe seems to know the ending to this joke. Everything back then…and then you have the audacity to act like you don't understand why I'm saying these things. Like really? You can't possibly be that damn oblivious."

"I get it. We didn't have it the way you wanted back then, but that was 12 years ago," I said my voice now a bit raised as well.

I watched her mouth open and close. As if she wanted to say something, but couldn't get the words out.

"Like I said, you have no fucking idea. You never did. Not then. And not now. And here you seem to think that because I'm doing my job, it changes all of that crap from before. It doesn't."

Stepping closer to her, I could smell her lotion, and what she used in her hair. Her eyes wide, but there was a storm brewing there.

"So, tell me what it is I don't have any idea about."

"You have no idea how much pain you caused me. The day all that happened, and you said all those things, they were all seared into my memory. Your parents, and the…"

"The what?"

"Nothing. It doesn't matter. All I'd be doing is opening up old wounds. And since I have to work with you right now, it wouldn't be wise."

I wanted to touch her face. Hold her in my arms then. Even with her angry, I wanted her so bad. Wanted to feel her lips again, wondered if they tasted the same. She was the only person who could ever make me feel this way, and I closed the small space between us until I was right in her face. There was always a bit of her pulling away even when we were in college, but I wasn't going to let that slide this time.

"Is it fair to compare who had the most pain?" I asked.

"No. I guess it's not." She sighed.

"If it helps, you can tell me. Maybe then we can really start fresh," I said with a twinge of hope.

"I will eventually. Right now, I can't. I...I don't think I'll be able to handle that kind of emotion right now." She stood up then, seeming anxious to get away from me.

"I still would like to have dinner with you," I said.

"And I still don't think it's a good idea."

"It is just dinner, Leah."

"Is it?"

"If that is what you want, yes. I won't make you do anything that you truly didn't want to do. We can eat and talk. No strings."

I touched her face then. I couldn't help myself. I ran my fingers down her face, and I could hear her breath almost stop. She trembled a bit in my arms, and I leaned in to kiss her, but she put her hand on my chest stopping me.

"Fine. What time?" she said, backing up.

"How's eight?"

"Sure. I'll see you at eight."

"Just email me your address and I'll send a car for you."

"You know I could meet you there."

"I will send a car. No ifs, ands or buts. I swear no funny business."

"I'm going to hold you to that."

My phone vibrated on the table, and I groaned inwardly.

"Until later Leah, my belle," I said with a wink.

"Until then," she said softly a sad smile on her face.

I walked out of her office, heading down to the car that I knew was waiting for me with my father in it. And even he couldn't ruin the smile I had on my face.

Chapter Fifteen

Leah

I finished the final touches on my article that was due and

sent it to the assistant managing editor of the magazine. Mel

was a stickler for deadlines, as she said she ran her editorial

ship in tip-top shape. I wasn't about to be on her bad side for a

missed deadline. I've seen it before and it wasn't pretty.

Besides, I had other things to do and I was thankful today was

an early day.

I was going to get my hair styled and nails done as it

was a normal ritual of mine that allowed me to feel good and

pamper myself. It might have seemed pretty minimal to other

women, but for me, it was something that was well needed. It

was something that made me feel complete when it came to

life's little pleasures. And since I now had a date to go to, I

guess it all made sense.

Grabbing my bag, I set up for an Uber and made my way past Dana's office.

"Dana, I'm leaving for the day. Just text or email if something important comes up," I said.

"Sure. How did the interview go?"

"It went well. Adrian…he was fine. Answered everything with no objections."

"Good," she said. "Was it as hard as you thought it would be?"

"Yes and No. I don't know. Not really. But he talked me into having dinner with him."

"Talked you into? You aren't usually one for being talked into anything."

"Says the person who talked me into doing this in the first place."

"That's different."

"If you say so. But I don't know. He kept pushing the issue, so I agreed. Maybe if we talk or something, the whole thing with him won't feel so unfinished. Maybe then I could really move on from all of it." I shook my head. "You know what, it doesn't matter. It's dinner. Nothing more."

Dana laughed. "And now it is my turn to say if you say so, Leah. See you tomorrow. Have fun."

"Sure thing."

I made my way to the Uber and waited as he set the GPS to my salon. Taking out my phone, I texted the address to Adrian. I found myself worrying about my appearance and what we would talk about. I had hoped he would keep the past where it belonged. We weren't going to do anything. I knew that, but still a girl wondered.

Once I made it to the salon, I told my usual stylist to put some curls in my head and make it look snazzy.

Two hours later, my hair was done and I looked great. I asked the stylist to pin my curls up so I can let them loose later on. After that, I made my way to the salon next door to get a mani and pedi. This time I would even change up the color a little to spruce things up. I didn't know who this woman was. I wasn't a woman who did anything for anyone but myself, and yet Adrian comes strolling back to New York and it hit me that maybe I was doing some of the things I normally do differently for him.

There was a part of me that thought he looked damn good in a suit, but then the other part of me wanted to prove to myself that I wasn't that same person from back then. He didn't have the power over me that he did before. Sure, it was only dinner, but I wanted to show him what he gave up that day all those years ago. I was different now. Stronger. I knew I was.

But then even as he gave those answers to those questions, I found his presence to be a bit much. It was always a bit much. Too much for everything. Especially me. I didn't need to get consumed with him again. I did that before and I didn't want to repeat that same song and dance.

After my fingers and toes were painted in a pretty pink, I decided to head home and shower. I covered my hair so it wouldn't get too messy and then find something to wear. Once I was done with my shower, I stood in front of my floor length mirror looking at how much my body had changed. I was still a bit on the slim side, but thicker in places I wasn't in college.

I grabbed my favorite lotion and rubbed it over my body, my mind wandering to Adrian. Picturing his strong hands rubbing the lotion on me. My insides quenched. I shook my head, trying to rid myself of any images of Adrian and me. The one thing I didn't need was to dredge that up no matter how good that part of our short-lived relationship was.

I decided on a tight black dress and a shawl to cover my shoulders. I received a text from Adrian that the car was waiting for me downstairs. Once I reached downstairs, I realized that it was a limo and not a car.

He was showing off.

I wasn't complaining, but a limo wasn't necessary. The driver drove down the streets of Manhattan and as expected, the traffic was horrendous. I shot Adrian a quick text and put my phone back in my purse closing my eyes. I was tired. Already it was a long week, and for me, my week wasn't over. I still had work to do to finish this article about Adrian and then I would go back to my research for another piece I was doing.

Almost 40 minutes later, the driver pulled up to the back of a restaurant by the water. The driver got out of his car and opened the door for me.

"Thank you," I said absent-mindedly surprised how beautiful this place was. This seemed much more than a simple dinner date. As I walked up to the door, it opened and there was Adrian in his very best suit, smiling at me. I was astounded, at how good he looked. Really good. He was wearing a navy blue suit, with a white shirt, no tie. The top two buttons were open on his dress shirt, and his suit blazer was open. His long hair once again tied up. He came to me, his hand extended. I took his hand and he led me into the restaurant. I could see that we had the restaurant absolutely to ourselves and I was pleasantly surprised.

Once we reached the table, he pulled out my chair. He lightly grabbed my arm to stop me from sitting.

"Leah, you look amazing. Like wow. Or rather damn!" he said with a smile twirling me around to check out my body in the dress.

"You think so?" I said, surprised that came out of my mouth. It reminded me of how I was with him in college. The Leah, who always wanted to outshine all the other girls who wanted his attention.

"I know so."

"Thanks. You look really nice yourself. Really nice."

"Just nice?"

"You look good, *Adrian*. But I'm sure you know that."

"No. I don't. Or rather I just want one person to think about how good I look. I'm honestly surprised that you didn't change your mind. I thought you would've thought it over and decide to not come."

"Why would I do that?"

"Earlier you were upset. I know how you can be sometimes with holding a grudge."

I laughed at that. "That is partially true, but, Adrian, I'm fine. We're good. Thanks for asking me to dinner."

He let me sit down, and pushed my chair in. For a moment I felt he was two different guys. Sometimes he was super egotistical in college. It damn near came out of his pores, but then other times when he wanted to make things special, he did. Now, it seemed he was only the guy trying to make a good impression. His ego seemed to be a thing of the past. He was more mature now. Maybe it was because we were both older than we were then. But I liked it. I wasn't going to complain.

"This is a nice place. I don't know why I've never heard of it before."

"My dad owns it and the view is magnificent."

I fought back any of the negative things that came to mind about his dad. Instead, I said nothing at all.

I glanced in his direction and saw exactly what he was talking about. Our tables faced the water and the city outline. It was absolutely breathtaking and I gasped.

"This is beautiful," I said.

"It is. Though it isn't as beautiful as you."

"Oh? Is that one of your pickup lines" I said my brow raised.

"No. I wish I could say that it was, or rather I would say something a lot better if I used a pickup line. But it is true.

You are the most beautiful woman I've ever had the pleasure of laying my eyes on."

"Thank you," I whispered softly.

There were so many things that I wanted to say. So many things that I wished I could've said before. But I didn't. I didn't think he needed to know now anyway. It didn't matter at the moment. I studied his face. It matured. His goatee. His body. I realized there was a part of me that held on and that was why I was so angry about doing all of this. In all the time that had passed, I hadn't moved on. Not really.

"What's on your mind?"

"Nothing much. My mind's always busy." And that was true.

"I would say I believe you if I didn't know you. But I do. You wear all of your emotions on your sleeve. And from the far-off expression you have on your face right now, I would bet that I'm right. You're thinking about something."

"It isn't important."

"I don't buy it."

"You don't have to. It really isn't important. Just a simple revelation," I said with a shrug.

"Is it about me?"

"Yes."

"What about me?"

You still do things to me that I wish you didn't. I may even still love you.

"I'm telling you, it isn't serious. You just seem all grown up now." I said instead.

He grinned widely at that. "Is that a bad thing?"

"Of course not. Don't be silly. We all have to grow up sometime."

"So our chef is making us herb chicken, roasted potatoes, grilled vegetables, and other fixings. I hope that's okay with you?"

"Still trying to take charge I see."

"Well, it's more of a habit now. You know running the hotels and stuff."

"Except, you were always that way. Trying to put your foot down and what not. Like I was just supposed to do whatever you said because you were Adrian Kai Mahina Robinson. Superstar football player in the making," I said jokingly.

He chuckled. "I mean I was one, in college at least. I admit some of that was because I was used to getting my way and getting what I want. And then I wanted you. You were stubborn in college. Stubborn as hell. And I see you as a challenge. I never turn down a good challenge."

I cocked my head slightly to the side. "You say that in present tense?"

"That's because even now, 12 years later, you're still a challenge. You're stubborn, but I like that. But I'm sure someone as inquisitive as you are would know that. You probably know more about me than I think you do."

"Any particular reason you believe that?" I asked.

"You're a reporter. It would be strange for you not to."

I thought about what he said and he was right and wrong at the same time. True, I was a reporter and when I needed to find out something about someone, I did whatever I could until I did find that out, but with him, I tried hard to keep distance. I made sure I didn't look him up. I didn't want to know what he was doing or who was he doing it with. Nothing.

"Well, I hate to burst your bubble, but I don't know much about you and your life now outside of what I found out from my research for this article, and what I knew before. It was much too painful to follow along with what your life was. I didn't want to seem stuck. Though now that I think about it, I'm quite sure that I'm pretty stuck because I didn't even want to see you at first. I don't know what it is with you, but it was hard to pull myself away from you. And when I finally did, and things seemed like okay. I finally was able to tell myself that I got this, and then here you come back in my life because of my job. I mean, what are you supposed to do when that kind of thing happens?"

He was quiet for a moment as if he was thinking and then he reached over to grab my hand. "I would say that maybe fate has led me back to you because that is where I belong. Fate wants us together."

I didn't know what to say to that. He almost told me what he was thinking, but I didn't know what to say. So, instead, I said nothing.

Our food was bought and we ate in silence. My mind was elsewhere, but it didn't stop me from sneaking looks at him. I pretended to be interested in the view, but that wasn't the case. He was just so damn sexy. He went from the boy with the slightly long hair in a football jersey to the man that knew how to fill the hell out of a suit. We finished and I sipped my wine slowly wanting to make sure I had a clear head.

"Come with me," he said. He held out his hand for me to grab.

Instead of me arguing some point that wasn't necessary at the moment, I obliged him. We made our way to the balcony that separated us from the water. It was a gorgeous view. The city's skyline and the clear sky. It was almost picture perfect. He held my hand and I didn't pull away. I was so conflicted. My head was telling me to leave the past where it belonged, but my heart was telling me there was something unfinished there. Something I had to do. *We had to do.* But how do I do that when there was so the one thing he didn't know?

"You know I thought of nothing for years but you. Your smile. Your eyes. Your beautiful body. The quirks and even when you were upset with me. I felt like when you left me, you moved on without me and without ever thinking it would be different. But even though I know a good part of everything had to do with the fact that I was an asshole back then, I still hoped."

"And now?"

"Ever since I found out that I would be able to see you again, I have been patiently waiting to get you alone. Get you alone and profess my feelings. Rather, what I've been feeling this whole time. Tell you that what you said to me that day was true. I never forgot you. It was hard. No matter whoever came into my life, it was always you I thought of."

He gripped the railing of the balcony, his voice firm.

"We both have jobs to do. I know that. But it doesn't change what I feel. What I want with you."

We stood side by side looking out at the water, which was peaceful, unlike my thoughts. I could sense that even though we stood next to each other, he was watching me.

"Yes?" I said not even looking up. I guess we were still somewhat in tune with each other.

"Look at me."

And as always when he made a command, I found myself listening, even when I wanted to fix my mouth to say something smart, I didn't.

His hands, touched my face carefully, his eyes searching for something, but of what I didn't know. His left hand touched my chin, tilting it up for me to get a better look at his face. He leaned in slowly and our faces were so close to each other. I could only hear the heavy thumping of my heart. My heart that was unsure, but the same heart that wanted to feel his lips again. I closed my eyes, and his lips brushed mine and I sighed as he kissed me softly. And just as I was about to relax, his cell phone vibrated in his pocket. He pulled away from me annoyed, and another expression I couldn't place on his face.

"Saved by the phone call," I muttered, but he didn't hear me.

"I'm sorry," he mouthed as he stepped away. I nodded.

It was probably for the best that nothing went any further. I was sure that if anything did go further I wouldn't have told him no. And considering I still had a job to do, there was no need in messing that up for a simple romp in the hay. Granted, it would've been a damn good romp in the hay. But it didn't matter. Not anymore and while he took the phone call, and stepped away, I realized that I did have feelings for him more than I was willing to admit, and that was something I wasn't mentally prepared for. The biggest issue was telling him the one thing he didn't know. Tell him that there were little things that reminded me of how things ended before. How in the end when I really needed him to, he didn't choose me. And I wasn't even sure if after all this time with the changes he seemed to have made, would my heart be willing to be put on the line again.

He came back in, and I forced a smile. I was out of my league again. It wasn't that I didn't think I was good enough.

It was that I wasn't sure if I could do this again. Do anything that could lead me back to the spiral we were in before. He would push, hard at times, and I would pull denying that I had an attraction for him. Denying that there were things I felt with him, I never felt again. My biggest issue was losing myself again in him. I couldn't do that. Not again.

"Are you okay?" he asked concerned.

"Yep. I'm fine," I lied.

"You know I always know when you aren't being honest with me."

"Yeah. But I'm fine. No worries." I said. I smiled brighter this time hoping he would take the hint. He did.

"Sorry about that. There is always business to attend to. It seems that it never ends sometimes."

"I understand. You're a hotel mogul. It sounds like you'll always be needed," I said, my voice sounding much sadder than I wanted it to.

What the hell was wrong with me? It didn't matter what he did with his life. Once, this was all done, he will go back to running his empire, and I will go back to doing what I do best. Writing and research. Get the truth as much as I could out there. I didn't have time for the past to catch up to me.

"Should I get you home?" he asked, his tone different, but unreadable. He probably knew that I was lying, but I didn't owe him anything anymore. We were not together.

"Yeah, sure. That would be fine."

Adrian held out his hand and I took it as he led me back to his car. It was a Mercedes and for some reason, it fit him. It fit the new him.

"I thought I should drive you home unless you want the limo to take you back."

"You can drive me home."

The ride home was silent, as I found myself feeling extremely tired. By the time Adrian had reached my home, I was sleeping.

"Wake up sleeping beauty," he whispered near my ear leaning over me. I opened my eyes to see his eyes sparkling with amusement.

"Tired?"

"I guess more than I thought I'd be. Thanks for dinner and for driving me back."

"Anytime. That is what friends are for."

"Yeah... friends?"

"I think we're more than that."

Once again, I didn't have a response, because I suspected after it all, we were a little more.

"I'll call you in the morning, so we can work out the details of the photo shoot."

"Great. Good night Leah."

"Night Mr. Bachelor," I said with a smirk.

He laughed and I watched him get back into his car. A part of me wanted to call him back, to maybe come back upstairs with me, but the other side, the more rational side decided against it. Memories are nothing but dying leaves floating in the wind. Once they fall, they are meant to stay on the ground and blown away. They aren't meant to be put back into the branches they fall off of. And so I took myself to my apartment alone with my thoughts of my life and him.

Chapter Sixteen

Adrian

I sat at the small restaurant near Battery Park with my mother

for lunch. She had come up to New York for the opening, and

have insisted that I have lunch with her. It was a beautiful day.

The sun was shining, and I was happy.

"You have been avoiding me," she said, interrupting

my thoughts.

"I haven't. Things have been a little intense these days

you know what the hotel opening up and what not. You know

that's always how it is," I replied.

She took a sip of her tea, her brow creased, in deep

thought.

"Your dad tells me that you've been in contact with

Leah."

I exhaled. "She's doing a piece for her magazine. You know, for the eligible bachelor's thing. It's also great promo for the hotel."

"Uh huh. And that's all?"

I couldn't help, but smile. "No. You already know I have feelings for her. I always had. I'm sure I always will.

"Do you even know what she has been doing all of these years?"

Confused, I put my fork down. "What do you mean?"

"Did she tell you anything about what happened after you got hurt?"

"Yes. She finished school in New York and now she works for a magazine. Why are you so curious about her all of a sudden? I was under the impression, that you didn't like her."

"No reason," she replied. I couldn't help but feel she was asking for a reason, but I couldn't figure out what.

"How are classes going?" I asked.

"You know summer classes are always a breeze. Fewer people in the classroom. Less stress when it comes to grading and giving assignments."

I nodded. She used to always say that when she taught at the high school before. Now she was the history professor at Ocean View.

"Do you plan on rehashing anything with Leah?"

"Mom, why are you asking so many questions about her?"

She put her fork down and touched my arm.

"You're my baby boy. And even though my marriage to your father was short lived and unhappy, I got you out of it. You're the best thing of my life, and my greatest gift. I worry that you'll be hurt or taken advantage of. I know you're grown now, but it doesn't change a mother's worry," she said.

Weighing in her words, I couldn't think of any kind of rebuttal for what she said. I was happy my mother still cared this much about me, even though my dad always held me at arm's length.

"Do you plan on capitalizing on this whole bachelor thing?"

I shrugged. "I don't know. It wasn't like this was planned. It was a nice surprise. I'm not sure New Yorkers care too much about this kind of thing on an ongoing basis. They want the things they pay for to be worth it, and that is my hope. If this bachelor thing helps that though, I won't be against it," I said.

"That's what I want to hear. My son making the right decisions."

"I can do that on my own mom. You and dad worry way too much. I can handle what I need to."

"You seem to think with your other head when it comes to that woman."

I sighed. "Leah, you mean. She has a name."

She waved her hand flippantly.

"Anyway, she's a distraction. Even now, you rather spend time with her then handle your business."

"My business handling skills are fine. And no matter what you or dad says, I'm going to continue to spend time with her. I know how much you like to control things, but in this instance, I don't need you to," I said firmly.

My mother said nothing, as she continued to chew. I knew she had more to say, but I didn't want to fight with her. There had to be a way I could get my mother to see that Leah wasn't a bad person. If I got my wish, I would have Leah be more of a permanent fixture in my life. My parents didn't understand that she made me better. She always has.

Chapter Seventeen

Leah

As the camera shutters clicked, I watched as Adrian looked in

his element. As the magazine's photographer took photos of

him for the spread, I found myself thinking about him in all

the ways I shouldn't have. Wanting his hands all over me.

Wanting him to make me feel better, even if it was only for a

moment. It has been a long time since I had sex and the last

time I saw him, I wasn't sure how long I would've been able

to hold out if he kept on looking as good as he did.

His hair was tied back in a ponytail. His goatee was

trimmed nicely and his brown eyes sparkled with mischief. As

I watched the other women that were in the room, I knew that

they thought the same thing I did. He was as fine as sin. Hands

down one of the sexiest men I'd ever seen. I thought he was

handsome in college, but there was something different about him. Almost dangerous, and I didn't know if I had the strength to make sure I didn't find out what that was. He had my heart in a tizzy as I watched him pose changing up between serious and a smile. He was the perfect bachelor on paper. Handsome, changed career paths and succeeded, had his own money and did I mention handsome? No, I didn't care about all those kinds of things. It wasn't my style to worry about those kinds of things, but I was surprised to learn that he didn't keep doing sports related things. Most former athletes would become a coach or sports analyst. But Adrian did a complete 360. I knew how much football meant to him back then. It was one of the things that tore us apart. He used to always say how nothing would make him happier than pass rushing on the field, and defending for his team. It was so complicated, but sometimes it was easy.

The photographer made a couple of comments to him as I texted Dana to let her know how the shoot was going. Usually, I wouldn't sit in on any of this. I wrote my article and went on about my next assignment. However, for some reason, Dana wanted me here and Adrian had also made it clear that he wanted me here too. I already knew what he wanted, but my issue was that I didn't know what I wanted. I was afraid. Plain and simple. I didn't want myself disappear for any guy ever again.

Looking back up, I saw that Adrian had taken his shirt off. Donned in just slacks, I could see just how good his ass looked in them. His dark wavy hair now laying past his shoulders onto his back, and my mouth involuntarily opened, my mouth all of a sudden much too dry. *Fuck, I needed some water.*

He gripped the football tightly in his hands, and that's when I noticed the tattoo that he had mentioned before. It was huge and magnificent. And all I could think about was running my hands across his back.

I could hear one of the women in the room whistle and I rolled my eyes. Didn't she have a job to do? And the more I looked at him, and the admiring stares from the other women around the room, I got more and more annoyed. Why the hell was his shirt off anyway? Did the magazine really need him like this? He was showing way too much, and I glared at him from across the room, as he did all the photographer asked him too. Another woman cheered and I turned my glare to her. Why were they acting like they've never seen an attractive man before? Even as I said it, I knew why. They knew what I knew. He was the kind of man you look at and wished that he had you in his hands rather than the pigskin he held.

I turned my attention back to him, realizing that I was jealous. Jealous at all of the attention he was getting.

We made eye contact. He gave me a wink before turning back to the camera giving that winning smile, and I shook my head. I decided to get that drink after all. I wasn't going to pay the shoot any more attention, even if doing so killed me.

Once the shoot finished, Adrian made his way to me, his shirt still open.

"Do you plan on closing your shirt?" I asked him, pointing to his bare chest.

"Yes, I wanted to make sure you didn't run off," he replied buttoning his shirt.

"What do you think, boss?" he asked me, a playful smile on his face.

"It was good. Though, I'm not sure why they had you take off your shirt. I don't recall that being part of what was planned."

He chuckled, his eyes lighting up. "No, but the photographer thought it would be good to have some of those shots. I was told they would use a picture of me from when I played in college too. Something like a comparison shot.

"I guess," I said, trying my hardest to sound unbothered, but failing miserably.

"Why? Did it bother you?" His face was questioning, but amused at the same time.

"Of course it didn't bother me. I was just surprised. That's all. You seemed to be getting a lot of attention from the women in the room. It almost reminded me of how the girls acted around you when we were in college," I replied.

"You definitely sound jealous."

"You're wrong, I'm not."

He got closer to me. So close that my ass was pressed against the table, and my chest pressed against him.

"If that is true, you wouldn't be looking at me with daggers right now. Actually, if it didn't bother you, being this close to you shouldn't bother you either," he said.

"Wrong again." I tried to keep my expression mutual.

"Or maybe you're mad because I didn't come over here sooner. Give you all of my attention."

"Yeah okay. Keep telling yourself that."

"I think I'm right."

I laughed louder than necessary. "No, you're not."

"So, if I put my hands around you, and you'll be completely unfazed?"

"Yep," I replied, not sounding as confident as before.

His fingers lightly touched my face, and when they touched my lips, on cue my eyes closed, expecting his lips to brush against mine. That, I would feel his hands on my face, his tongue prying my mouth open.

But there was nothing. Confused, I opened my eyes again to him looking at me smugly. Trying to save face, I pressed my hand against him to move his body away from mine.

"Is anything wrong?" he asked.

Narrowing my eyes, I shook my head. "You're an asshole."

"Am I?"

Ignoring him, I rolled my eyes. "I had a momentary lapse of judgment." He shrugged then.

"If I remember correctly, you weren't too happy with that kind of attention back then either." He was bringing the conversation back my jealousy.

"I didn't care. I knew being a good football player came with attention. I didn't, however, want to be goaded or having girls try me once they figured out we were a thing. It was annoying and aggravating and you ate the attention right on up. Almost like you thrived on it. It was just... ugh!"

"Of course I liked the attention. I was always one to want to be in the spotlight back then. Can't fault me for that. I'm not like that too much now. Now, I am doing it because it comes with the job and it comes with the name. I'd rather be behind the scenes now. It is much more to my liking." His voice was sad momentarily, and then he shrugged.

"I have to sign some papers and make a few calls. But the opening is next week. I want you there with me at the opening. Would you be my date?"

"Your date?"

"Yes. You know when two people decide to go out on a night on the town together."

"Stop being a smart ass. I know what it means, I just don't know if it's a good idea."

"Why not?" he asked with an amused look on his face.

"Frankly, I don't think it would be appropriate and I really don't want to be on any gossip rag. Because if any of those reporters are like how I am, they will find out that we dated in college and I rather not have that splattered all over the pages of New York's magazines and papers."

"Oh, so now you care about what other people think?"

"Yes and no. I don't normally care. I just want that part of my life in the past. Not thrown back in my face. It isn't anyone's business."

"Oh, I see. You're ashamed of me," Adrian said with mock hurt his hand playfully on his chest.

I rolled my eyes. "Oh, stop. No. I'm not ashamed of you. Why are you being so weird? Fine, I will go. What time do I have to be ready this time?"

"The hotel opening ceremony is next Friday night. It's in the early evening. There will be a party afterward. All the people involved and those who invested etc. My parents will be there, but don't worry, it won't be an issue for you. I rather know that I have someone in my corner who won't bore me to death with details that aren't really appropriate for a party."

"Okay, Adrian. I will be there. I assume it is a black tie kind of event."

"Yes. You are correct, my lady."

"Fine. Fine. Well, let me get back to the office. I have to do my final read through and finish another assignment."

Adrian moved closer and I could see the eyes of all the women in the room, and I wanted to melt into the carpet. Don't get me wrong, I normally didn't care about attention, but for some reason, I didn't want anyone to know about

257

anything concerning Adrian and me. More so I rather we had conversations in private where they would be less time for people speculating about things they had no clue about.

"How about afterward I'm done with what I had to do today, I pick you up and take you to my place out here?"

"For?"

"I want to hang with you a little. Enjoy your company. Is that too much to ask?"

"Um…okay. I guess," I said dryly. Pick me up around seven that way I'll have time to get out of my work clothes."

Adrian smile widened. "I can help you with that," he said.

I laughed. "In your dreams, Adrian. That isn't what I meant. I will see you at seven. You already have my address." And with that, I walked out of the room refusing to turn back around. I wanted him to watch me walk and let those other women be jealous.

Maybe I was a little jealous. Maybe it was because he looked so damn good while he was being photographed or maybe it was more of the fact that I still had feelings for him after all this time, regardless of the pain the end of our relationship caused.

Later that evening, I glanced at the floor length mirror at the navy blue dress that I wore. I didn't know what Adrian had in mind, and I don't even know why I agreed to it in the first place. But I had to admit that it was nice spending time with him after all this time without wanting to kill him. I guess you can say that time had matured me for the most part.

Right on cue, the doorbell rang, and I grabbed my purse and opened the door. Adrian stood there in dress pants and a dress shirt sans the suit jacket. His hair was tied back up and I looked him up and down with much appreciation.

"You look beautiful," Adrian said. He took my hand, twirling me around.

"Thank you."

"No, thank you. Seriously stunning. I can't wait to see what you'll wear next week. I can't guarantee I will be able to keep my hands off of you though."

"Oh really?"

"No promises," he said with a wink.

We stepped out of my apartment, and I locked the door before following him downstairs to the black Mercedes he had parked in front of my building. It was a beautiful car, and I was glad that there wouldn't be cameras trying to see what was going on as they surely would've if he had come to get me in a limo. Once we made it to his apartment building, we rode the elevator to the penthouse. He, of course, had this floor and the one below it for privacy reasons. I was surprised about how nice it was for such short notice. It was classy but very manly. He had leather couches and a chair with a wide tv that was mounted on the wall. He had a nice rug in the middle of the room, and a couple of paintings here and there. I could tell his place needed some more personal touches, but for the most part, it didn't seem like the typical bachelor pad that was barely lived in.

"Your place is nice."

"It's coming along. I feel like something is missing though," he said with a casual shrug.

"Like what? You have a fantastic view and I am sure you will make more changes to this place once you get more settled."

"What I had in mind wasn't a thing, but rather a person." He looked at me then something in his eyes I couldn't read.

"And who would that be?" I asked him already knowing where he was going, but wanting to actually hear him say it.

"You."

"Why would you want me here?"

"Because I believe that good or bad life happens the way it does for a reason. There is a reason we are back in each other's lives. Sure, the article thing was the original reason, but both of us are seemingly in good places. I think there is a reason for that."

I raised my eyebrow. "Maybe I'm just being nice to you. After all, I haven't seen you in years, and I am technically on assignment."

He shrugged. "Or maybe you are feeling what I am feeling. Maybe you are just denying it."

I raised my eyebrow, a smirk on my face.

"And before you say something sarcastic, know that I know you. I know how you operate for the most part."

"You haven't known me in a long time, Adrian."

"Do you think that much about you have changed?"

"Yes," I said indignantly.

"Sure, maybe you have a little. But I don't think you have that much. Maybe you're doing what I've known you to do. Acting like you're not fazed by me. Maybe you want me just as much as I want you. As much as I wanted you since I saw you again. As much as I wanted you since forever. I never had another woman like you. No matter how pretty she was, she wasn't you. No one had your personality, your charm, or sounded the way you sounded when we made love. Those kinds of things you can't replicate. You can only hope that the universe will bring that back in the cards for you, and make sure that now there is a second chance, you don't fuck it up.

"Who said I wanted a second chance of anything than what it is?" I said, my throat suddenly much too tight.

"You didn't have to. Your body says it. Your voice says it. I don't know if you realized that your voice raised a little. And your body isn't as straight as it was, almost as if you're more relaxed. I could be wrong, but I was never really that wrong with you. At least I'm pretty sure that I wasn't."

I didn't say a word because he was right and I didn't want to tell him that. He didn't need any more encouragement, but even as those words played in my head, my body as usually betrayed me. *Talk about being loyal.*

"That doesn't necessarily mean that. Maybe it just gives us a chance to heal and then move on. Maybe that it all it is a chance to move on and close the door behind whatever it was or whatever relationship it was."

Even as I spoke those words I knew that it was more than that. I knew that. It was much more than just closing the door on old wounds. It was almost as if we were meant to cross paths again. Fear wouldn't let me willingly take that chance. Part of me wanted to tell him what really happened the day we officially broke up. After another moment I decided that now wasn't the right time.

"I think you don't want to admit that. And that's fine. I know how you are. You're stubborn. Your stubborn streak is one of the things I loved about you. I still….I just don't want to lose out on what could be different with the two of us."

Adrian closed the space between us and I could smell what seemed like peppermint on his breath. He grabbed my waist and pulled me close to him, and my heart quickened. I knew that I wouldn't be able to tell him no. I didn't know how to tell him no. Now all of me was feeling all jumbled up and confused. My body responded to just being around him. I knew that if he kissed me, we would end up in his bed. Was that a chance I was willing to take?

"Leah, I missed you so much. So much," he whispered.

"I don't think this is a good idea, Adrian," I said, my voice so soft that I wasn't sure if he heard me.

He leaned towards my face, his lips so close to mine that I could feel his warm breath. I closed my eyes, knowing that I wouldn't turn him down. I couldn't. I felt the lightest tap on my lips, a gentle brush that fluttered over them. I kissed him back slowly at first, feeling dizzy with all kinds of emotions. I pulled away to look at him, trying to read what was on his mind. But he pulled my face towards his, his lips tougher now, needier, as he crushed his mouth against mine. The kiss between the two of us became so intense that I had begun to feel weak in my knees. The warmth of his mouth sent a warm current down my body, and I shuddered in need. His tongue rolled around my mouth and I relished it all. It felt wonderful. I needed more.

"Please let me have you," he said, his voice husky.

I lowered my arms and took a deep breath. I clung to his shoulders and opened my eyes hesitantly to look up into his eyes. His dominate stare was so intense, that I wanted to look away, but for some reason, I couldn't. He pulled me to him with his stare alone. I wanted this crazy attraction that we had between us to stop, but I knew it wouldn't. It was much like it was before. And after thinking of all the reasons I should stay far away from him, it was then that I realized I never really stood a chance. He still had my heart, so any reasoning was futile. I opened my mouth trying to say something, but there were no words. I couldn't find my voice. It was a feeling I had experienced with him before, but not to this extent. It was heavy. Intoxicating. It scared me. I was afraid I would fall apart again and in the wake of that, there would be nothing left for there to be picked up.

He was an addiction. A drug. My favorite drug. And I knew that if I took a hit of it this time, I wouldn't be able to quit. I was lucky the first time. I couldn't risk a relapse because what if I couldn't let go this time?

He placed his fingers gently on my chin, lifting my face to his. And the doubts I had about wanting him started to waver. My body and mind were on the same page. He lowered his lips to mine. It was so intense that I gasped, my body damn near collapsing. He held me firmly, his tongue moving around in my mouth, and I moaned. I was not winning this. He pulled away, his gaze hungry.

"If you want to stop now. I'll stop. But if not, let me have you. Let me make love to you. Touch you in ways that you have never been touched before. Love your body in new ways."

I let all that he had said roll around in my mind, before finally responding.

"Yes," I said with a soft nod.

He picked me up by my ass, his hands gripped my cheeks, as he brought me to his bedroom. His hands were still big as I remembered, but they felt different, more in control.

Placing me down on the bed gently, his eyes roaming my body as if he was memorizing every part of me. Lifting up my dress, his fingers traced the outline of my thong, and I squirmed once his fingers gently caressed my pussy. Leaning over my thighs, he took in my scent before letting his finger trace over my clit. His finger flicked over my folds, and then slowly one of them slid inside. A strangled moan left my throat, making me sound like another person. I had been wet for him since this afternoon, even after I showered and played with myself thinking of him. I was wet and dripping with a need so bad, that I grinded on his finger. He slipped another one in there, bringing me back to the first time we had sex.

The same hooded look in his eyes and my juices sliding down his fingers. His lips joined his fingers, as he sucked and moved in and out, his pace wilder.

I squirmed under his touch, my moans becoming louder as I clutched the sheets. This was torture, and I already knew that I would come quickly as I reached my climax. Adrian's tongue was buried in me as I let out a sound I never let out before, the waves of pleasure washing over me. He continued long after I had stopped shaking and I couldn't take it anymore, pushing my hands against him to get him to stop. He seemed satisfied with my response and smiled.

"I missed the way you used to come for me too. I think I want new memories, though." He stood up, taking off his shirt and pants and walking over to the dresser near the bed. Opening the drawer, he pulled out a condom and made his way back to the bed. Once he was out of his briefs, his dick long and wide stood at attention and I found myself watching him, not remembering him being this big before.

Rolling the condom on, he paused before sliding into my warmth. I let out a long sigh as he slid inside of me, causing me to grit my teeth in pain and then pleasure. He groaned before he started to thrust, moving slowly at first teasing me. As soon as he got inside, I was ready to come all over again, and I let him know that by grinding up against him so he could go faster. As his pace quickened, I made a guttural noise of approval. He took it as a way for his thrusts to become deeper, as he watched the ecstasy on my face. I clutched his ass, as he moved in and out, crying out for more, the Lord and other things that weren't coherent. This is when we worked best together. We were two bodies that fit perfectly like a puzzle. We were always in tune when sex was involved.

Adrian groaned as I tightened around him, my legs following suit. I screamed his name over and over, my vision becoming hazy as I came again. He pounded into me before coming as well, letting me know by the animalistic sound coming out of his throat. Sweat trickled down his face and he gasped, his hair no longer in a ponytail.

"You're amazing, he said. He placed a kiss on my nose and laid down beside me.

"Wow," I said softly.

"Is that a good wow?" he asked.

"Yes. I missed that. I missed you even if it pains me to admit it."

He chuckled. "I want another shot, Leah. Can we try again? We can take it slow."

"I don't know."

"You don't have to decide right now. I just now that you are mine, and I am yours. I always have been. Always will be. And I won't give up on you or on us."

I nodded. It was all I could do. I was tired. Drained, but in a good way. I snuggled against him, my mind wandering in a million places, but my body winning as I fell asleep.

Chapter Eighteen

Adrian

The next morning I woke up to the sounds of the classic

oldies playing. It wasn't blaring, but loud enough that I could

hear the faint traces of it from the bedroom. Looking to my

right, I could see that Leah was no longer in bed with me. And

I was reminded of last night, the way I wanted to have her in

so many ways, and the fact that I stopped myself. Everything

was perfect. Much too perfect, but for some reason I wanted to

prove to her that I was different than I was before. Different

than I've been in a long time. And most of all I wanted her

back. All of her. Mind, body, and soul.

I know she got used to taking care of herself. She was

always so stubborn and feisty. It was so many things. I thought

back to how she was the calm in the storm back then. When I

thought about how demanding my father was, and how

emotionally abusive my mother was, she was the only thing that anchored me. She gave me some kind of peace. I glanced at the little note that she had left on the side of the dresser.

Wanted to go for a jog, and then work out for a bit.

Leah

I decided to go look for her and that was when I realized she was downstairs in the workout area of my apartment. I walked down the stairs and saw my beautiful Leah focused as she punched the punching bag hard. Her muscles were toned, and each time she punched the bag, her muscles flexed just a little. It was both amazing and sexy that she was so into working out now. The smell of sweat penetrated the air. She wore a sports bra and shorts, her hair tied up by a hair tie. The expression was one of determination and fury mixed into one. I marveled at the way she moved with such focus. And as I watched her, I realized that there was something else that I loved about her. Something that made her who she was. I wanted to wrap my arms around her and pull her down to the floor, her body sweaty, and mine willing to get that way if I could have her again.

All of a sudden she stopped and looked at me a sheepish look on her face.

"Hey. Sorry, did I wake you?"

"No. You didn't. I woke up realizing you weren't next to me.

She looked down at the floor, her eyes avoiding me.

"I'm glad that I didn't wake you," she said.

"Did you sleep okay?" I asked.

"I think so. I had a lot on my mind. One of the reasons I'm doing this, but otherwise it was okay. You?" she said.

"Better than I have in a long time. "

I wondered what that meant. I know we still had so much to talk about, but a part of me was delaying the inevitable. In my heart, I felt that whatever she had to say would be the end of what I wanted with her. From her. And I was being selfish because I wanted her all to myself. All of her. And this time I wasn't letting anything get in my way of that.

"I'm going to take a shower. Do you want to join me?" she asked me.

"Is that really a question?"

"Who knows? Maybe you would change your mind, and want nothing to do with me. Or maybe being in a tight space like a shower, would be too much for you and you would want to keep your distance. I don't know. Just thought I would ask."

"You? Naked? You don't even have to ask."

Making our way upstairs, I went to the bathroom to turn the water on and then stepped out to get extra towels. By the time I returned, she was in the shower, the water pouring over her and instantly I was hard. Fuck. This was going to be much harder than I thought. Her eyes were closed and I could see that she was in deep thought. Stepping into the shower behind her, I watched the water run over her body, and her ass and it took everything in me to hold my composure.

Once she had finished her shower, she got dressed. She seemed lighter. She hummed a song I wasn't familiar with, her eyes sparkling. Unlike before. I didn't want this to end. I followed behind her and once I reached the kitchen, I clicked the coffee machine so I could have some coffee. After the

274

shower, I didn't want to do anything at all but to stay with her, touching her body, and make her let out the sounds she made when she was in the shower. She smiled as the sweet aroma of coffee filled the air.

"You know I used to hate coffee, and then I started working at the magazine and realized that it was almost a necessity. Smelling this right now is giving me a warm and inviting feeling if that makes sense. It's like crack in a cup. I am addicted now."

"You can always be addicted to other things."

"Yes. And if I recall correctly, I was addicted before. Addicted to you actually. And well, you know how that went. We were no good for each other."

"We were young."

"And dumb."

"But in love."

"Or lust," she counted.

"Are you telling me you didn't love me back then?"

"No. I…I just know that I gave my all to that relationship and then it ended and I was left trying to pick up what remained of my broken heart. It was too much. Too much. Not enough me in there."

"And if things are different now?" I asked.

"Different how?"

"I am not the same immature boy I was in college."

She nodded, but said nothing else, and even after what happened last night, she was still keeping her guard up.

"Are you really that scared to try again? What if things could be different from them? We were stubborn college kids. We didn't really know what life really was."

"I don't know. I mean you're right, we didn't know. I guess that was being naïve. It doesn't mean that we have to open up past wounds or open doors that were meant to be closed. It just isn't necessary. I don't think I even see the need for any of that."

I paused.

"Are you telling me that you didn't feel any of that last night? It was passionate. We were perfect together. We weren't perfect back then. I know that. Believe me, I lived with the mistakes from back then. We both are stubborn about how we want things to be and how we expect things to be. But I can't go another day without trying again. You're the only woman I've ever loved. I want to see if we can work. I don't believe that we were too wrong for each other to try again."

I watched as Leah twirled her hair, biting her bottom lip as she thought about what she said. Even after all this time, she still bit her lip. She still did so many things that reminded me of back then. But there were things I was finding out that were new about her. I was okay with that though. I would do anything to prove to her that I was ready to be the man I wasn't when we were younger. And age was only partially to blame.

She sipped from the cup and then nodded.

"Okay, Adrian. I mean I would be lying if I said that I still didn't have feelings for you. I do. But we need to take things slowly. And we need to make sure it doesn't become that vacuum that it was when we were younger. I need you to promise me that. It won't be like that. We will have a healthy relationship this time."

"I promise."

She gave a small laugh that was mixed with amusement and a little pain,

"Don't make promises you can't keep," she said quietly.

Standing up I went over to her and held my hand so that she could take it. She stood up and I pulled her in my arms. "I don't intend to."

"Are you ready for next week?"

"I am. I haven't been this excited about a hotel opening, ever! I think having you on my arm makes it even better."

"It's surprising. How easy we've fallen back into old habits."

"You say that like it is a bad thing."

"It isn't."

"You could sound more enthused," I said.

Leah rolled her eyes. With exaggerated happiness, she clasped her hands together.

"Yes, Mr. Robinson, it's such an honor to be in your presence," she said laughing at the expression on my face.

"You just love being sarcastic?"

"Yes. But so do you. And a pain sometimes."

"I can't control that."

"What a bunch of bullshit. You can if you want to." She had this amused expression on her face. I kissed her then. Enjoying that it was no anger between the two us. We were truly enjoying each other's company.

"Maybe I can change your mind about that," I said a wicked grin on my face.

"I need to be decent and coherent at my meeting today. You're lucky I was able to even get a workout in this morning, after last night."

"That means I didn't do my job properly if you were able to get up without any issue," I quipped.

"Believe me you did!"

I kissed her again enjoying how good her lips felt on mine.

"Let me head home. I have to get ready and I am sure there are tons of emails that I need to answer."

"I'll see you later?"

"Yes."

Leah walked out of the room then and I watched as she got dressed.

"See you later, babe," I said a bit absently as I saw my father had called many times. I already knew it was bullshit. It was probably not too important. Or not as important as he had made it.

The day of the hotel opening, I made my way to the conference room at the back of the new hotel. Dad planned on going back to Miami after this. Business as usual. I sometimes wished that my dad and I had a better relationship. But I was starting to think that would never happen with the two of us. It was always the same thing with him. Work, work, work, and nothing else. I don't even know how at any point my parents even had time to have a relationship, let alone have me. He was always putting that over us. Except when it came to me being a part of his hotel empire. Then, he didn't know how to let go.

"Today's the big day son. How are you feeling about all of our hard work finally coming to fruition?"

"I feel good. We did it. And I'm going to run one of the best hotels in NYC," I said.

"The very best."

"Sure, dad. Was there a certain reason you wanted to meet here? You called so many times that I thought something was wrong?"

"Well," he paused for a moment pacing slowly as he did whenever he felt what he had to say was really important.

"What's going on with that Leah woman?"

"Leah?"

"Yes."

"Does that matter?"

"When you're running an empire, it does."

I sighed heavily, trying to control my temper. My parents were always doing this and meddling in things that had nothing to do with them. It drove me fucking crazy.

"What happens between Leah and me doesn't concern you. Why don't you understand that? What I do in my personal life doesn't concern you." I was angry and I had to clench my fists to calm down.

"Are you supposed to be this eligible bachelor? How would that look to those who felt that you were successful enough to be a bachelor? Bachelors are supposed to be single and uninvolved. I'm sure there are pretty other suitable women you can be involved with after this hotel has been open for some time," he countered.

"I'm a grown man and I can be with who I want. I don't get you and mom. I don't see what your big issue with Leah is. What did she do to you?"

"You have no idea of the trouble she could have brought you back then."

"What are you talking about?"

My dad looked at me with disdain, but didn't say anything. I knew that meant either because it was he felt there were more important things or that he would talk about it later.

"Once the ribbon is cut, I want you to make your way around the room and mingle. New Yorkers can be brutal, but we are going to show them that we got what it takes to handle business here just like we do in California and Miami."

"I got it, dad. I got it. I have to start getting ready," I said, my tone even.

"Be on time," he said, but I was already on my way out the door.

I reached Leah's apartment at five and I went upstairs to get her. I rang her bell, feeling nervous all of a sudden. I never felt nervous normally, but for right now waiting for her to open that door made me feel nervous like I was a high school kid or that guy who sat with her alone for the first time in college.

Leah opened the door, and I knew my mouth dropped open. She looked stunning. Her hair was pinned up and she wore a long black dress with a slit that went up to the mid-calf. Her breasts were pushed perfectly, showing just enough cleavage.

"Damn!"

"Is that a good damn?" she asked.

"Most definitely it is a good damn. You look so damn beautiful, Leah."

"Thanks. You look pretty damn good yourself."

"Only for you."

"That's not what the magazine says," she said with a wink.

I knew she was referring to the bachelor thing so I laughed.

"Well, the only woman I am looking for is you." Grabbing her hand, I waited as she locked the door, and we headed down the limousine. Her hand was soft and I could smell her perfume, and I was tempted to take her back into her apartment and have her again. But I had a hotel to officially open and I was glad that even if I couldn't have her in the way I wanted, she was with me as my date.

Once we were in the limo, she laid her head on me, her eyes closed. When we were in college, she used to do that after a stressful day or when she had a lot on her mind. It was her way of calming down or relaxing if I was there.

"Are you okay, babe?" I asked her.

"Yeah. I'm just worried. I don't want to feel like I am going to mess up your big night."

"Worried about what?"

"Do you want me to be honest?" she said.

"Of course."

"I don't want to be around your parents. All of my memories of them are bad. And again the press knows how to put two and two together about things they want to find out. I write for a magazine. I know how it goes. I don't really want anyone mentioning our past."

"I'm sure it'll be fine."

"And what if they ask about the two of us? What am I supposed to say to that?" she said. A small line of worry appeared on her forehead.

"Are you ashamed of our relationship?"

"No. It's just I'm not used to people worrying about those kinds of details. It's usually the other way around. I find out stuff and report it. Not people asking me questions. You were once a college football star, turned hotel magnate. That is a story right there. A big one. One of success. And then with all the hoopla with the fact that you made the top ten of the world's most eligible bachelors, that is something else that they will be asking. The fact that my name will be on all the articles attached to this special edition we are doing will have people talking. I just don't want to deal with all of that. It doesn't mean that I am ashamed of you." She turned to stare out the window.

I took in the words she said completely understanding what she was saying and what she meant. In my world, it was good to keep as much as you could private, but I wanted the world to know how much I loved her. I've held on to my love for her since the day she walked away. And I let her, all because I wasn't strong enough to stand up to my mother. I couldn't handle all the stuff that was going on with my career back then. I didn't want to make that same mistake again.

"Leah, I understand why you're worried. I won't let you be in a situation that makes you uncomfortable. I love you and I want the world to know. I see it like this, they can know about you and know of our relationship, but they don't need to know anything else. And I know we never said anything about if we are actually in one again, but what I said still stands."

Leah smiled and laid her head back on my shoulder. I kissed the top of her head and we were silent as the limo drove through the streets of Manhattan. I would've been lying if I said I wasn't a little nervous about tonight.

"I know this is a big night for you, Adrian. Don't worry about being under your father's shadow. You're going to be great. This hotel is going to be great. You got this."

And as if she could read my mind, she silenced all my worries.

Twenty minutes later, we made it to the hotel. Grabbing her hand, I walked with her to the entrance of the hotel. There were cameras, press and other reporters taking photos and trying to ask questions. My father had already prepped me on what the right words would be to say and to keep my answers short and sweet.

Someone in the crowd called my name, and I turned, pulling Leah with me as we smiled for the camera. Another camera flashed and I pulled her in for a kiss.

"That'll get them talking," I said with a wink.

"Wouldn't that mess up this whole bachelor thing?" she asked me with a small smile on her face.

"Maybe. But it doesn't matter. I've already told you. I'm taken. Or maybe it will raise my clout. Some women like a man that is already taken. It means there's something about us."

"You don't need me for that. Obviously, women already feel that way about you. With all those shirtless pictures that were taken, I'm sure that is enough for the women to go off of. They don't need me for that."

"True. But again, none of that matters. None of it. I got you, babe!"

We made our way through the room, and I ran into Ryan, the manager of this hotel. He was a hard worker and had managerial experience from before. He was one of the few people that my father recommended that I hire, and he made a good impression on me. He was a tall, somewhat lanky man, with reddish hair and blue eyes.

"Hey man, what's up?" I said.

"Hey, Adrian. It's the big night. How are you feeling?" he replied.

"As expected. It doesn't get bigger than New York City. This is the mecca of the world. It was only right that we had a hotel here too. How are you feeling?"

"Good. Thanks again for giving me the opportunity."

No, thank you for working with me. I need all greatness on my team."

At the moment Ryan looked over at Leah and smiled.

"Who is this beautiful woman on your arm?"

"This is Leah, the love of my life," I said. I could see Leah's cheeks flush.

Ryan raised his hand to take hers, and as Leah raised hers, he pulled her in for a hug. If I didn't know how Ryan was, I would've been mad.

"Leah it is nice to meet you. I'm Ryan. I don't know how Adrian was able to pull a woman as gorgeous as you are, but luckily he's a good guy or I may have to steal you for myself."

Leah laughed at that. "You're much too kind. It's nice to meet you."

"Hey, big man!" I heard behind me and I turned around. It was Tommy. Even after all this time, we were still as close as we were in college.

"Thanks for coming man," I said, giving him a pound and a hug.

"Leah! You look great. I would be lying if I said that I haven't been following your writing career. I used to hope you would use your sass to maybe mention the team and the NFL and then I remembered how much you detested writing about sports."

Leah hugged him, laughing genuinely. "You look great. And that's still true. I've been following you as well. You're one of the top quarterbacks in the NFL. Big plus that you are great both on and off the field."

"And what is that supposed to mean?" I said jokingly.

"It means unlike you, when I first met Tommy, his tongue wasn't down my throat. He was always nice to me." She shrugged.

"She got you there, bro," Tommy said.

"He knows I'm right, that's why," she said.

"So, the two of you are just going to get together after all these years and gang up on me, huh?"

"Maybe," Leah said.

"I mean when a woman is right, she's right. How's Marcy?" Tommy asked, his expression hopeful.

"She's good. You should maybe hit her up. Have coffee or something. I don't think she will turn you down."

"Thanks. I'll keep that in mind."

Turning towards me, Tommy placed his hand on my shoulder.

"And you know I wouldn't miss this for the world. Look at you moving up in the world. Don't forget about us little people," Tommy said. His eyes twinkled with amusement.

"Says the NFL football star," I said.

Initially, after the injury I sustained in college, Tommy was one of the few people who didn't act like I didn't matter now that I wasn't useful. I couldn't quite get back to the way I used to be on the field. It was a rude awakening for me. And it made me appreciate the people I had in my corner even if that had diminished once I was hurt.

"Well, maybe. But this is something that can go on forever. Football isn't one of those things," he said, his voice low. It was different than his normal, cheerful self. I made a mental note to talk to him later on because I knew something was bothering him.

"We will catch up in a little bit. I have to find my father and get ready for this speech I have to give."

"Of course man," Tommy said with a nod.

I continued until I eyed my father walking towards me. He glanced at Leah, the expression on his face impassive. I knew he wanted to say something about the fact that she was holding my hand, but he would wait until we were alone.

"Glad you're finally here. I can see why you're late," he said.

Ignoring what he said, I gestured towards Leah. "Dad, I don't know if you remember Leah. I was picking her up. I had to have my woman here with me on this big night. Leah, you remember my dad right?" I said my eyes never leaving my father.

"Yes. I do. How are you?" she said. My father's gaze never wavered from me. It was as if she wasn't standing there.

"It's time for you to get up there and make your speech. The press has waited for you long enough," he said completely ignoring her.

I nodded and gave Leah an apologetic look.

"I'm sorry," I mouthed to her. She shook her head in understanding, but I knew she was peeved. It was evident in the expression on her face. My dad always knew how to make a person feel bad. It was a gift that he had.

Turning back to Leah, I squeezed her hand.

"Baby, I'm going to the podium. I will make my speech, have one drink and we can leave. I know I own this place and all, but I don't want to be here with all these stuffy people. I want to be alone with you."

"Don't you have to be here a little longer? It's your opening night ceremony."

"Ryan has it. All the paperwork is done. Money is paid. Investors, etc. I'll be fine."

She touched my arm then. "Okay. Don't worry about me though, I'm fine."

"Thanks, babe." I kissed her again and let her hand go so I can go to the podium. My dad was already there talking to the crowd. They looked at him in his expensive suit. He knew when to be charming, turning it on when necessary. It amazed me and pissed me off at the same time. My dad was a hypocrite.

"And now, ladies and gentlemen, I want to introduce you to my son Adrian Robinson."

There were loud cheers and clapping as I made my way to where my father stood. I waved at the crowd. It almost felt that I was in politics the way the crowd was reacting.

"Thanks, everyone for being here. I wouldn't be in this position if you all haven't welcomed me and my family with open arms. There are plenty of well-known hotels that have been New York staples for years. You all have a certain expectation for quality and the best that a hotel has to offer.

With The House of Robinson, you will get that plus more. I want you all to have a top-notch experience. It doesn't matter if you are having a small staycation or you're a tourist coming to New York City for the first time, and want to take in the sights. I want you to walk out of here refreshed, happy and feel like this place is part of your family. Ryan Miller, who will be the manager here, is one of the best hotel managers I've ever seen. Our staff is impeccable. We plan to make our mark here in New York and I thank every single one of you for believing in my vision. I can't wait to leave a mark and hopefully make history in being one of the best damn hotels in New York City. Let's make history."

I finished my speech and there was once again loud clapping and cheering. I was already ready to go, wanting to get out of this suit and tie and back up under Leah. However, I still had rounds I had to make around the room.

As I stepped off the podium, I shook hands and posed for pictures. But I couldn't focus once I saw my mother standing there with Leah. My father was over there too, and whatever they were saying pissed her off. I could see it in her face.

Excusing myself, I made my way towards them. I could see that Leah was tense and she trembled slightly but said nothing.

"Leah...baby are you okay?"

Leah looked at me and then back at my parents.

"No. I'm not," she said quietly.

"What happened?"

"I was just reminding her of her place. That's all," my father interjected.

"And what does that mean?" I said.

"She knows what I mean. She knew what I meant before too."

Leah's mouth opened and closed. I knew her temper, and I didn't want this to escalate, especially not in here. I expected Leah to say something, but oddly she didn't. Instead, she shook her head and walked away.

"Dad, what did you say to her?"

"I told her the truth. I always tell the truth. ."

"Somehow I doubt it all went down the way you said it did."

"I told you earlier today, you shouldn't have brought her to the hotel opening. You have an image to uphold."

"And I told you that what I do doesn't concern you. Nobody cares who I date."

"This conversation doesn't need to happen here. Why must the two of you always be like this?" my mother asked from behind, confused about what was going on. She knew why we didn't get along. Sometimes I was sure she instigated things between the two of us. Besides, when it concerned things they felt were for my well-being, they usually were in cahoots with one another.

"Tamina, leave this to me and Adrian," my dad had said in an effort of putting his foot down.

"You two may cause a scene. You will not do this here," she said, her voice growled lowly.

"You don't know what I need or want. I can't believe you're doing this here," I said.

"Both of you stop it," my mother said, looking between the two of us. I had to remember where I was because I almost snapped.

"I'm proud of you. Proud that you and your father are getting along enough to work together, and even better you two are doing it in one of the greatest cities in the world."

She tried to change the subject. She was good at that when she wanted to get her way.

"Mom. Thanks. I'm glad you're here. But I can't have the two of you making problems for Leah. I'll call you later."

I hugged my mother quickly and left my father, walking out of the ballroom. I had to find Leah. As I knew she was going to let me have it. But even if she was angry, and took it out on me, I had to make sure she was okay.

"Hey," I sat down next to her.

"Hey," she replied.

"What happened between you and my parents?"

"The usual. They didn't want me here. Your mother was more subtle about it this time, but they still don't think I'm good enough to be around you. I don't know why either.

It's not like I'm some women from the wrong side of the tracks or I want your money. I have my own career as well. They hate me for no reason," she said frowning.

"They don't hate you."

"Are you really going to sit there and defend them after everything that just happened back there? Your father told me I needed to stay in my place right in front of you."

"I'm not defending them. I want to know what happened. I don't want you upset. That's all"

"Well, I am!" she said, her voice raised. Realizing that she sighed.

"I need to get out of here. I need to go home."

"Can we at least talk about it?"

"What for? So you can make an excuse for him? For both of them? You know, like you always do. Your mother didn't seem as bad as she did when I first met her, but she still has her feelings about me. I understand that they're your parents, but I've done nothing to them. The only thing I ever did was love their son."

"Baby, I know…"

299

"Don't do that! Don't pacify me."

"I'm not. I don't want to fight with you. I'm on your side," I said, loosening my tie. I was grateful we were alone. If any press got any info that I was having an argument with Leah, they would eat it up and not focus on the hotel.

"I just don't want to have to constantly deal with them and their crap. I don't know any woman who would want to."

"I get it. I know my father can be a piece of work, but he's mostly all talk."

I watched several emotions pass over Leah's face. There was anger and then hurt.

"You know what? Fuck it! I don't know why I thought it'll be any different with you. I'm leaving. You can either stay here or go with me, but I will not stay here and I will not act like I am okay when I'm not," she said wiping tears from her face.

And with that, she turned and walked away. I knew I would hear some shit from my father about leaving without doing all the things I needed to do, but Ryan was there and I had to make sure Leah was okay. For some reason, it felt like it was already the end of what was supposed to be our second chance of being together. And I couldn't let that happen. So, I called for the limo and followed her outside. She wasn't going to get away this time with closing up her emotions and pushing me away. I needed to know what happened. All of it.

Chapter Nineteen

Leah

We made it back to his apartment, and I was angry. Angry at him for not understanding why I was angry. Angry that even after all this time, his father knew how to get under my skin. I had hoped that I wouldn't have to deal with him, but sure enough, he had to spew his bullshit and because we were at his event, I couldn't say all the shit I wanted to say.

For a moment I had forgotten how it was when I was involved with him before. While the relationship with Adrian and I was a bit of a whirlwind, his father always made it known how much he didn't like me. How much he hated me. Now here I was doing with all the same kind of crap all over again. And I was mad at Adrian though I knew he did nothing wrong here. I just didn't know exactly what I was supposed to do with what was going on.

"Leah, what is wrong? You totally shut down on me."

"I don't want to talk about it right now. I'm trying hard not to say all the things that are in my head right now. I didn't want to deal with this shit right now."

"What happened back there?"

"Your parents!"

"What else is new? You can't let them get to you."

"Oh, so deal with their crap because they're your parents right? Got it."

"No, baby that is not what I'm saying."

"Then what the fuck are you saying then?"

He paused then, angry. But I didn't give a damn. I was angry and I wanted him to feel how angry I was.

"Leah, I won't let them do this anymore. Never again. You have my word. But I can't try to fix anything if you shut me out."

"You wouldn't understand because…" and I stopped myself. He wouldn't know because I had never told him from all those years ago, and I wasn't going to right now. Yeah, he needed to know now if I wanted this relationship to actually work this time, but there was a big part of me that didn't think it would go smoothly. He would probably react the way he did when it all went to crap before. And his parents would spin it. They always did. Adrian would fall for it. I couldn't have that. Maybe he wasn't that person anymore, but how was I supposed to know that now. I couldn't help but dwell on the conversation from earlier.

I watched as Anthony and Tamina walked towards me. Adrian's mother was dressed regally, and it was hard for anyone not to notice her in the room. Her eyes didn't seem as cold as they were the last time I saw her. Even though she was slightly older, she still turned heads. Much like her son.

I turned back to see Anthony standing in front of me. He still looked like the boss of everything. The guy who knew how to get what he wanted if need be. He had so much power and I was still angry about how he was responsible for the demise of my relationship with his son before. He changed my life that day, and I haven't forgiven him. Even if he denied it.

"Leah. I admit I'm surprised to see you here. I thought by now Adrian would've gotten over whatever spell you had him under," he said snidely.

"Spell?"

"You know I never thought you were good enough for him. He had his whole career ahead of him, and then you came along and distracted him and other unmentionable things."

At that moment I knew what he was referring to and it pissed me off.

"I did no such thing. Your son wants to be with me. It's his choice. I didn't force him."

"It doesn't matter. It didn't last before. It won't last now. He has a hotel to worry about. Besides that bastard child of yours is gone now anyway."

"Maybe I should tell him why that is."

"You can, but it won't mean anything. He won't believe you. I'm his father. We butt heads, but he'll believe me. You need to know your place."

Those words ate at me. I didn't want them to because I knew Anthony wasn't worth it, but it reminded me of that day I was robbed and beaten. Right after that, my relationship with Adrian ended and I went through all that pain alone, and it made me livid.

"Stop it! Please. I don't want to talk about it right now. I don't want to say something to you out of anger that I don't mean. I think we've done that enough to each other before," I said, nearly sobbing.

He ran his fingers through his hair, which was no longer in the ponytail he had earlier. And while he stood there debating if he wanted to let it go or not. I wanted to feel numb. I needed to. No thinking of what happened before or tonight. I needed something to take off the edge. Adrian was the perfect drug for that. I didn't care how it may have made the situation seem. For the moment, that is what I wanted. There was no room for any other negotiations.

"Kiss me," I said softly.

"What?" he asked.

"Kiss me, Adrian. I don't want to hear anything. I want to feel your lips on mine."

I could see the hesitation on his face. He reached up and then placed his hand back down as if he didn't know what he wanted to do. He probably thought I was testing him. I wasn't.

I went to him, and I ran my fingers through his hair. He was so damn sexy. Even in my anger, I couldn't deny that. I wasn't willing to talk right now.

"Please?" I asked him, my tone desperate.

As soon as our lips connected, every single emotion I was feeling, had come to life. I was so angry and aroused. And as all the vile memories of his mother came over me, he brought me back with his lips. They were delicious. And while he knew nothing of what had happened and why I was angry, I couldn't stop my body from responding. As his hands slid along my skin. Our tongues battled it out neither one of us wanting to back down. I knew he was angry that I didn't respond to him earlier. I was angry that once again I allowed myself to get caught up with him and this constant push and pull. I hated myself for wanting him. It was the same song and dance. I will pull away from him and he would pull me back, and while I know he did indeed act differently than he normally would, I couldn't help but feel like this was deja vu all over again.

Adrian picked me up and had me against the wall. His hands grabbing my ass the underwear I was wearing not even standing a chance.

"Why the hell are you so stubborn? What the fuck happened back there? What was that? I thought you said we would talk about whatever was bothering us?"

"I don't want to talk right now. Just fuck me or let me go home," I said angrily.

Normally I wouldn't want him touching me when I was in this kind of a mood. But that kiss and everything that had happened tonight had put me in a different place and I was pissed the fuck off. I needed to release in some way and I wanted Adrian to help me get there.

"Please, Leah…" he started to say, but I stopped that him by connecting our lips again. I sucked on his lip. He let out a long groan, his dick throbbed against my thigh. Still holding me in his arms, he carried me to the couch, placing me down on it.

"Take off that dress," he said, his voice sounded strangled.

I slid out of my dress, wiggling out of it, and as it landed on the floor, I watched him take his dress shirt off. He got out of his pants and stood there in his briefs and I could see his dick straining against his pants.

"You want me to fuck you? Open your legs."

I did what I was told a part of me liking this and another unsure of what I just unleashed within him. He perched between my thighs and then his fingers played with my breasts, his hands sending shivers down my spine. He tapped my legs for me to place them over his shoulders and I did. He licked and lapped down, causing me to gasp several times. I fell back against the couch, my body already writhing uncontrollably. He found my clit, and his tongue licked and sucked as I dripped into his mouth, my legs shaking long before I started to come. He kept me in place, as he continued, my hips grinding against his mouth wanting much more than he would be able to give me from his mouth. My eyes rolled to the back of my head as I came, his lips tugging gently at my swollen nub. I screamed loudly, as he pinned me down, letting me ride out the waves that rolled over me.

Once I was able to focus my vision on him, I could see his gaze was more primal.

"Turn around and raise your ass up," he said.

Trembling, I turned around and did what he asked. I was apprehensive, as I waited for him to do something. Anything. I knew he was making me wait. It was my punishment for earlier, but I didn't care. Not right then. Not at the moment. All I wanted was him inside of me.

"Leah," he whispered. "Are you on the pill? I want to feel all of you bare, skin to skin."

"Yes," I muttered.

"Good," he said. I could feel him get behind me, and I could feel my juices dripping down my leg. My breath was heavy.

I could feel him, prodding me a little, and then he rammed into me and I gasped. It was so intense and so good. And I screamed, my body feeling every stroke. He had set my whole body on fire, and the feeling encompassed all of me. I wanted to have some control, but he wasn't going to let me have it. I could feel his hair now touching me, and part of me wished I could have his hair in my hands, as he fucked me.

"Please baby. I'm right there," I stammered. And he answered me by thrusting into me again, and he made me go blank. His name came out of my mouth like a chant, low and guttural, as another orgasm ripped through me. The fire that he had lit burnt me as I screamed loudly. I was sure the whole building had heard me. Adrian squeezed my breasts from behind, as he pounded harder into me before he found his release inside of me. He shuddered against me. I leaned over the couch, totally spent and happy that I got out that release because it was so needed.

He plopped down next to me, putting a pillow on his lap. He gently took me from the side of the couch, and he laid me on his lap, his hand stroking the side of my face. There was still this dangerous look in his eye. I knew he was still pissed off with me.

"That was, uh…wow. Different, a bit dirty. It seemed familiar, don't you think?"

"Yeah. We've had sex angry before."

"I rather not be angry. I rather you talk to me and then we have mind-blowing sex," he said his fingers stopping for a moment.

"I don't think it would matter. I know how you are about your parents."

"How about letting me speak for myself. Don't assume. I'm not the same college kid I was back then. Back then I was immature, but I'm all grown up now," he said.

I sighed. "Your parents think I'm a bitch who ruined your life. They think you got injured because of me. Your mom made it clear years ago how she felt about me and how she thought I distracted you from your game. You thought that back then too. You all felt I was to blame for the injury when it broke my heart as much as it did yours. He told me to stay in my place. He talked to me like I was beneath him. It pissed me

313

off. It reminded me too much of before. You seemed like you were about to defend his bullshit again," I said fuming all over again. I was shaking by that point.

"Baby, I'm not doing no such thing. I just wanted to see what happened? I'm not defending them and I swear I will deal with them. Especially my dad. Okay?" Adrian said. His forehead was lined with worry and something else I couldn't quite read. I was sorry by this point that I took my anger out on him. It wasn't for me. It was for his mother. His father. It was for the bad memories I had attached to his family and for the things I had held on too for much too long.

"Can we just forget about your parents right now? I want to lay next to you and forget about them for now. Can I do that?" I asked him deciding that I still wasn't ready for having that conversation. I didn't want to mess up the rest of the night, especially after we sort of made up. It was also supposed to be a happy occasion since this was the night his hotel opened to the public.

"Of course, Leah. Of course. I don't mind laying with you," he replied.

"I'm sorry that your night didn't go as planned. I thought it would be best if I wasn't there so it wouldn't be a scene with me and your father."

"It's fine. I spoke. I made my rounds. It went fine. Don't worry or stress about it. You did nothing wrong."

I looked into his eyes, which were hazy from exhaustion, and I kissed the side of his cheek.

"Good night," I said.

"Good night, baby."

The next morning, I found a note from Adrian saying he had to go, but he would call me later. I looked at the clock and realized I had to get to my office. I had to finish up some minor things so that Adrian's spotlight would be ready to go for the next issue.

I took a cab to my house, showered, changed and made it to my office in about two hours. I had to make sure the spread on Adrian was perfect. And then Dana would give her final stamp of approval.

By the time the afternoon had rolled in, I realized I had quite a few text messages and voicemails. I checked them. They were all from Adrian.

Leah, we need to talk. It's important.

He said that a few times as if he was worried that I was ignoring him. I wasn't. I responded quickly.

I'll head over there after work. I got a small surprise for you.

The rest of the day went by pretty smoothly, but I couldn't shake that something was wrong. His messages seemed off, and I wondered if he really thought about what happened last night. Maybe he thought I was too much.

I made it to his office later in the day, and surprisingly so were his parents. Okay, this was weird. They all seemed so serious and another thing I couldn't fathom what they were all doing here.

"Hey, Adrian," I said cheerfully going to kiss him on the cheek. He nodded, but he was stiff and it made me feel off. Like he didn't want me touching him.

"Is everything okay?" I asked him.

"My parents told me something really interesting today," he said.

"Okay..."

"I was trying to figure out why you were so adamant about not bringing up the past, and then it all made sense."

"What are you talking about?" I said agitated.

"Leah, you were pregnant?"

My stomach dropped, heart racing. The room started to spin. The one thing that I didn't tell him, had finally gotten out.

"Yeah, but-"I whispered.

"You didn't think I should know about this? Know that you were pregnant with my child."

"No. It wasn't like that. I was going to tell you the day I found out. It was the day you got hurt in that game. I was worried about you. I felt it was best if you focused on your surgery and getting better. I mean you were sleeping, so I kinda told you. Of course I was going to tell you when you got up, but she wouldn't let me. I tried to tell you again, but that was the day you told me to get out of your life. You didn't

317

want to hear what I had to say. I tried. You believed what your mother had said. I was so angry with you. I left enraged. I wanted to hurt you. But, I couldn't. I took my grief and your words, and I moved back to New York. After all of that, I didn't think it was necessary to not tell you," I said quickly.

"Why not tell me afterward?"

"I believed what you said. I was angry. I didn't want to see you again. I wasn't pregnant anymore. It didn't seem that it mattered after that. The whole time you were there, your mother told me you didn't want anything to do with me. She made it as if I hindered your recovery in some way. But, I swear I wanted to tell you."

My eyes pleaded with him, hoping he'd catch on. Hoping he would talk to me in private.

"And you didn't think I should know even now?" he yelled out, slamming his hand on the table.

"Adrian, calm down."

"Mom, stay out of this!"

"No! I didn't. I didn't because I lost the baby. I went through so much after that. Alone. I had to move on," I said, shaking my head.

"You lost the baby? I should've known that. Maybe I could've helped."

"You didn't need to be involved with that," Anthony has spoken finally. I glared at him.

"Your mother knew. I told her. She knew. They both knew."

His mother came from around the desk where she sat. She came in front of me, her eyes cold and hard like I remembered them before.

"I thought it could've been someone else's. I didn't know at the time," she said smoothly.

"You didn't know?" I said sarcastically.

"You were the one who told me to get rid of it. You tried to pay me off. You told him whatever and he believed you. He believes you now. I can see it on his face," I said begging Adrian to believe what I was saying.

"As I said before, my son doesn't need you in his life. He has better options. He had them back then. He can have any woman he wants without your baggage," his father said callously.

"He didn't need mine, he has his own."

"I had plans for him. His mother wanted him to play professionally. Do you know what having a baby would've had meant at that time? He gets injured and then finds out he would've been a father? If he would've known, he wouldn't have finished school or gotten into the family business. I did what was best for him," Anthony said now in my face.

I waited for Adrian to say something. Anything. For him to come to my defense or at least understand. But he didn't. His eyes gave him away. They always have. Even when we were two stupid kids in college, his eyes always told me how he felt whether if it was anger, fear or love, it was like he couldn't hide that from me. And now as I watched the different emotions play in his eyes, I feared that I might have messed it up because I didn't tell him. But as I looked at the smugness on his father's face, I knew it wasn't my fault. It was then that I knew, what I had to do.

"You know what I thought it would be different this time. But it's the same thing. The only difference is you are all older, but obviously not wiser. Yes, I was pregnant and I miscarried. I miscarried in a horrible way. I had to deal with that alone. No, I didn't tell you, and I apologize. I'm sorry I didn't tell you. That is the only thing that you were right about. But I never wanted to ruin your chances. I wasn't trying to make it harder for you. But those were the damn cards we were dealt. As for you Anthony, I have a damn good career. I made my own name off of my work. I didn't need any of you to get where I have gotten in my career. I knew I should've kept my distance." I laughed bitterly then. Feeling nauseous and dizzy. I needed to get out of the office. I needed to get away from all of them. "Fuck all of you. Stay away from me. Don't worry, I won't be in your son's precious life. It's the same damn thing all over again."

Remembering that I had the mockup of what the article would look like, I pulled it out of my bag and gave it to him.

"Here! It came out great. I'm sure it will bring more attention to you and your hotel. Your parents know a lot more than what they're saying. But if I tell you what I know, you obviously wouldn't believe me. You have a nice fucking life!" I said. I spun on my heel and walked out. I didn't let the tears fall down my face until the door closed behind me. I made it to the nearest garbage can and threw up.

Adrian had been calling me nonstop for two weeks. I glanced at my phone and saw another incoming call. There was nothing left to be said. He picked his side. I spent enough time crying and wallowing in grief for a relationship that should have never started again in the first place. I watched my heart once again get stomped on because of his meddling parents. Meddling parents that stirred up shit one time too many. A small part of me wanted to know what he had to say or what he had to say. But it didn't matter. I had to get used to the fact that once again I let this happen. And maybe this time it was for the best.

Chapter Twenty

Adrian

The hotel had been running smoothly. The numbers were great in the first week, but I couldn't even focus on that. My mind was on Leah. I missed her. I didn't understand why she kept her pregnancy from me after all this time, but I still couldn't keep her out of my mind nor my heart. I called many times, but Leah refused to answer my calls.

The week after the hotel opened up, my mom came into my office. I glanced up at her, but said nothing. I didn't want to hear any more of her nagging about Leah. She got what she wanted so there was nothing else that needed to be said.

"Good morning, son," she said. Her voice was soft, a far contrast to how she normally spoke.

"Hi, Mom. I can't chat right now. I'm busy."

"I wanted to talk to you about the pregnancy situation."

"I think you and dad did enough. Leah is gone, what else do you want? I couldn't become this big football star. You got mad about that. Dad was already mad that I wanted to play, and once he realized I couldn't go pro, he wasted no time getting me into the hotel business. That was the only thing that was good enough for him. I had the one woman who I loved since 2004. I get another chance with her, and both of you made sure it wouldn't work. Again. So, mom, tell me, what else can I do for you? You want me to sign something with my blood? You tell me!"

I was livid. I paced the floor of my office.

"I understand that. But I'm your mother and you will talk to me with some respect."

"Respect? The things that came out of your mouth weren't respectable so I don't want to hear that shit right now. And it isn't about you being my mom. It was never really about you."

"I need you to listen to me."

"Like you have listened to me over the years?"

"Leah did tell me she was pregnant. The day you got hurt. When you had your surgery, she came there. I could kind of tell. I guess a mom always knows. She seemed different. Leah confirmed my suspicions. I was angry though. You got hurt and couldn't play in the Peach Bowl. It would've been your ticket to the NFL. I was mad that your father gloated that you could leave football alone. But I did tell him and he told me that he would handle it. I thought she took the hint. I heard nothing after a while, so I thought maybe she did what I suggested or, maybe she had the baby and chose to stay out of your life like I asked her to."

"What are you talking about?" I shouted not caring if anyone heard me.

"Stop raising your voice son. We are in a place of business," my dad said smoothly walking into my office and shutting the door.

"I get that you're partially invested in this, but this is my office and this is my hotel, I do what the fuck I want to do. Mom was telling me you had something about Leah and the

325

baby. What did you do?" I asked. I hadn't been this angry in a long time. I was angry with Leah for keeping this a secret for so long, but my parents? They topped that.

"I did what any father would do to protect his son and his investments," he said coldly.

"Investments? I'm your son. Not a stock or business deal. You talk about me like I'm some piece of property."

"I hired two people to handle it. They were supposed to rough her up a little. They were to make sure she didn't have the baby. She didn't want to take the money and get rid of it. So, I helped it along. It helped that she disappeared eventually. I didn't want you tied to a baby when you still had your whole life to live."

It was quiet then. You could hear a pin drop. My mother turned to look at him, her hand over her chest, and surprise on her face. I realized then that even she didn't know how cruel he could be.

"You did what?" I said, walking over to him and grabbing him by the collar.

"You hurt Leah. You killed my child because of some investment, I didn't even know was there. I'm your son and you can hurt me like that? If I wanted a child, or if Leah decided that she did, what did that have to do with you? You had no fucking right. No right. I can't believe this." My fists tighten as I held him against the door. He started to choke, but I only saw red.

"Adrian! Please. He isn't worth it. Let him go," my mother said softly from behind me. I ignored her. Holding him to the door, not caring anymore. Not caring that he was my dad. What kind of parent would do that to their own kid?

My mom was crying by then, but I didn't care. I wasn't going to console her. I finally let go of him. I knew that even if they weren't together anymore, she would be devastated if I hurt him or went to jail. He coughed holding his throat.

"Maika'I no au. I'm fine." It was a lie. I was far from fine. I've never been this way angry in my life."

"I don't want anything to do with either one of you. Who knows what else you manipulated, but you won't be doing that with me anymore. Get the hell out of my office. And, dad, your idle threats about you being in charge don't work here as this is my hotel," my voice coming out choked.

My father straightened his tie before walking out and slamming the door.

"I'm sorry, my son," my mother had said, her face wet with tears. She brushed her hand over my face.

"Mom, please...leave. Even if you didn't know about what he did, you were part of this from the very beginning," I said going to my desk. "You watched over me like I was your husband and not your son. I could've had keiki of my own. You guys took that away from me. I need to be alone. Maybe one day I'll forgive you, but I can't right now. Just go! Please!"

She nodded. I sat down. She turned and walked out of the door. As soon as the door closed, I let out a scream that resembled a wounded animal. My father ruined any chance I could've had back then at having a family of my own. Having Leah the way I always wanted. And she eluded to that, but I couldn't face it. I hurt her again. And now I had to make it

right.

Chapter Twenty One

Leah

Near the end of summer, Dana would always throw a

reception for the end of the magazine season. And the start of

a new one. For her a new year would start in the fall, so she

showcased the best pieces during the reception. It was also to

give a sneak peek into what was next for the magazine. This

time there was the big piece that I did with Adrian. The

interview, photos and the background article into him and

what his hotel brought to New York. It was a big hit with

everyone. For Dana, it was the confirmation she needed for

me to also do softer pieces while still remaining the writer I

was for the magazine.

I knew Adrian had to be here. It was unfortunate on

my end because even though some time has passed since that

day with his parents in his office, I was still mulling over it. I didn't want to be reminded about my heart being broken once again. I couldn't.

Marcy came up to me in a fabulous red dress and pulled me in for a hug.

"These are always so nice. I loved what you did with Adrian's piece. You almost talked as if you guys were good friends."

I laughed sarcastically. "We're not friends. I was doing my job," I said, lying to her and myself.

"Uh huh. Whatever you say," she replied with skepticism. She was on the right track. I was angry, but I still knew that I had feelings for him. Eventually they'd go away, but for now, I couldn't think that far ahead. I was still pissed at what went down. At him.

"Have you spoken to Tommy yet?" I asked, changing the subject.

"Yes."

"And? How did it go?"

"He wants to meet up with me before he goes to training camp."

"Are you going to actually follow through this time?"

"I think so. It's just hard you know," she said with a shrug.

I nodded and hugged her again. "Yes. I do know. I know it all too well."

"Can I have your attention please?" Dana's voice carried over the room from the stage.

"I want to thank all of you for making this another successful year. I couldn't have made this magazine shine the way it does without all of you. Every writer, photographer, editor, all of you. Thanks so much. Now, before we finish partying, I'd like to introduce Adrian Robinson."

I didn't even realize he was there already, but as he made his way towards the stage, I couldn't take my eyes off of him. He wore a black suit, with a black shirt, his hair tied into a ponytail.

"Wow! Time has been good to him," Marcy said, causing me to turn towards her. "What? He looks great."

333

Shaking my head, I looked back at the stage, as he looked around the room. Once he found my eyes, he wouldn't look away. Part of me wanted to move away from his gaze, excuse myself and go to the bathroom or something. Anything. But my feet stood planted onto the ground feeling all the things I didn't want to feel.

"First, I wanted to thank Dana for reaching out to me to do the article. It has been a tremendous help with my hotel. And I am forever grateful," he said.

Dana raised her glass as a thank you. And he smiled before continuing.

"I also want to thank Leah Hunter. Many people didn't know before this, but we went to college together. And while I could tell so many stories of our time at OV, I will stick with how much she has grown with her writing. She put me in a light that I frankly don't deserve. She wrote the article, effectively and efficiently, and the questions she asked were perfect. She's perfect. I've never met a woman like her. One who fights to get what she wants and works harder than anyone I've ever encountered."

I could feel the eyes of some of the attendees, but I kept my eyes on Adrian. Feeling that I would cry in a moment. Not, for what he has said, but because of the whole situation.

"Leah, I owe you an apology. I should've listened to you and sometimes I'm pigheaded and stubborn. But, I also know that having you in my life brought sunshine that hasn't been there in a long time. You make me laugh and think, and I couldn't let any more time go by without telling you that."

Marcy grabbed my hand and squeezed it. "That is the sweetest thing, I've ever heard," she whispered. Maybe it was but I couldn't hear anymore. I needed air.

Adrian looked around the room, his champagne glass raised. "I wanted to thank all of you for allowing me to be part of this and for including me in the latest issue."

With that, I turned and headed straight for the door. I needed time to process what he'd said. I made it to the elevator and pushed the button frantically, feeling as if it was delayed on purpose.

As the elevator doors opened, I got in and saw Adrian getting closer. But just as the doors were closing, he reached it putting his hand in the door. The doors opened back up, and he got in standing on the opposite side of the elevator. We were on the top floor and 20 stories up.

"You don't have to talk. I want you to listen," he said.

"I don't particularly feel like listening either," I said, looking down at my feet. Anywhere but at his eyes. I couldn't look at him. He would break my resolve.

The elevator made a funny sound and then it stopped. This couldn't be happening. Of all the times it would be to get stuck in an elevator. Here I was stuck with him. This stupid, devastatingly handsome, heartbreaker.

An alarm went off. I covered my ears and sighed.

"Damn it," I muttered. A static sound went through the help box near the button panel.

"We will get you guys out of there. We already called for help. Just sit tight," I heard a man's voice say.

The alarm had stopped, but I was still in this confined space with Adrian. I didn't want to be here. I didn't want to be with him at all. I was adamant about that.

"I'm sorry," Adrian said.

"It doesn't matter anymore," I said, closing my eyes. "I don't want to hear any apologies."

"I'm sure you're probably tired of hearing me apologize, but it doesn't change that I'm sorry. I truly am. I didn't realize how cruel my parents could be."

"What do you expect me to say? I told you so?"

"No. I don't expect you to say anything."

"Then why follow me into the elevator."

"Because... Aloha au ia'oe."

I shook my head remembering what that meant. "You don't love me. You're holding on to some piece of your past. That's it," I said coldly.

Adrian closed his eyes tightly as if he didn't want to hear what I said before he opened them again.

"You and I know that isn't true. I love you because I always have. I always will. I know what I feel. I know what I felt back then too. Even if I have to make a fool out of myself to prove it, I will."

"You should've done that then with your parents. You chose not to believe me," I yelled.

"You're right. At the time, there were too many questions. I truly didn't think my mom would lie to me and manipulate me. I was angry. I wanted to throw something. I felt defeated and helpless. I knew I took it out on you, but I felt if I spiraled, I couldn't have you spiral with me. But I couldn't do that. Not to you, so I said nothing."

"And that's nothing new!"

"I know."

"In college, we were addicted to the fact we were so different from each other. Addicted to the way our skin felt against one another. How high we felt when we were entangled in passion. That isn't love. It's borderline obsession. Nothing more. Or at least we were with sex."

I could see him get angry then. His eyes fierce, but steady. I knew it was stupid to hold on to that anger after all this time. Especially since he hadn't known. But the way he said nothing still haunted me. His betrayal had festered in my chest, and I watched him, his expression conflicted.

"I'm not going to respond to that. Not while angry."

"You don't have no right to be angry, Adrian. You did this. I gave you everything before. Everything. And you broke me. You took it all and left me with nothing. I wasn't enough. It wasn't enough for you," I said yelling, hot tears falling down my face.

"You know, while I might have always been on my best behavior back then, you have a tendency to run. You run when things seem to hit too close," he said.

I put my hands over my face to avoid looking at him.

"Don't do that. You know it's true. You also know that as much as you had hoped, things didn't change. We both thought all this time apart would make us hate each other. But it didn't. It's still there. Stronger than before. It was in the way we kissed. In the way we made love. In the way you looked at me when you thought I wasn't paying attention. It never left us, Leah. And I'm surer now than ever that it won't ever leave us. We're meant to be together. Be in each other lives because it wasn't all bad. You know I'm right too," he said, pleading with me.

It was something I had wanted to be gone for years. I knew when I kissed him again, he wouldn't stop trying to stake his claim. He would break me. Like the last time.

"What's different now?" I said, my voice small.

"I was immature then. I didn't know how to fight for you then. I was going through all those emotions of not playing, and I listened to my parents. It was wrong. I know that now, but that's what happened. It doesn't mean you weren't enough. You were more than enough. I didn't deserve you then. His eyes were soft then.

He closed the space between us, taking my shoulders in his hands, his grip firm.

"You know life isn't great until you can share it with someone you love. I love you, Leah. And I'm sorry. I'll spend every single day for the rest of my life trying to show you how sorry I am. Sorry that I didn't do the right thing back then and even when I should've recently. I won't ever do that again. You are what I want and what I need in my life. I don't care about my parents. I know what happened. I know what they did. And when it hit me that we could have been something, that I could've had been a father and married to you all this time, I was enraged.

He paused then, the muscles around his eyes were tense, his expression pained.

"I love you so much. But back then all I could think about was the football career I left behind. This hotel thing came about because I was good at it, but it wasn't what I wanted. And then after all this time, to be around you again. To see that you did everything you said you would do, I just…I'm so fucking proud of you. I swear it's just me and you. I will protect you from anything. From anyone. I will never feel whole again if you aren't by my side. It's not enough. I need you to be mine again. I fucked up more than once. But I can't be without you. I can't eat or sleep or breathe. I wake up with you on my mind. You're the best fucking thing that has ever happened to me. I'm yours. Always. Mau Loa. Even the last time I saw you back then, and those last words you said to me. I never got you out of my head. Forgive me for my mistakes. Please? "

A hefty weight of anger had started to lift. I had wanted to forgive him, but I was so stuck on him not being there when I needed. Stuck on him not letting me be there for him.

"When did you find out what really happened?" I asked.

"About a week or so after. I missed you the same day you walked out of the office, but you wouldn't return my calls. They told me, well he told me what happened. How he went out of his way to hurt you. I can never take that pain from you," he said.

"I don't need you to."

Adrian let my shoulders go, putting his palm on my cheek. I found myself sliding to the floor of the elevator, all of this being too much at once. He slid down with me, pulling me onto his lap. He kissed my head.

"I never stopped loving you. Not for a minute," he whispered, looking into my eyes. His touch tender, gentle. I could feel the fire sizzling off of his skin. You got me to this point. I thought of you often. Your smile. Your voice, the way your fingers would slide across my skin. Those memories kept me going."

"I'm scared," I finally said.

"Don't be. I got this. We got this. Things aren't supposed to always be beautiful. Sometimes they're ugly. And that's okay because that's how life is. And I want it all. The ugly, the beautiful, the in between. All of it. And if we drown, then let us."

I said nothing after that, putting my mouth against him. We kissed like it was for the last time. His tongue was fierce, quick, as he groaned against my mouth."

The elevator started back up, and I pulled away shaking my head. I stood up first smoothing out my dress. Reaching over I put my hand out for him to take it, and he did.

"I love you," I said.

"I love you more," he replied. "Always!"

Chapter Twenty Two

Adrian

(2017)

We sat in the Skybox waiting for Tommy's first game of the season. The new NFL season had started, and Tommy invited me, Leah and Marcy to the game. I held a beer in my hand, my other arm around Leah.

She was smiling, her face glowing as she leaned her head into me. She had just told me last night, that she was pregnant. It was like everything had come in full circle. I got the love of my life back, and I had a new chance to be a father. I could go on and on about what happened with my parents, but it didn't matter. My ohana was right here. One, right next to me, and the other growing inside Leah's belly. My Leah was hāpai.

Leah wrinkled her nose at something, and I brushed the hair to the side of her face.

"Are you okay?" I asked her worried that she would have to run back to the bathroom.

She nodded. "Yes. I'm fine. For now."

We spent the whole night talking about it. Me, happy that she would bring a new life into this world. And, she worried about the fact that she felt sicker than she's ever felt.

The TV was on. Sports was on the screen, but it was muted. I checked stocks on my phone. Leah had been in the bathroom for a bit, but I didn't want to disturb her. She seemed on edge recently. I knew she had a crazy deadline to finish, but there was something else I couldn't quite put my finger on.

She came out of the bathroom, holding her stomach and gave me a weak smile

"Adrian, we need to talk," she said, sitting down next to me on the bed.

"Of course," I said, pulling her into my lap. I don't think I could ever get tired of doing that.

"I haven't been feeling well, so I went to the doctor. I'm pregnant," she said softly.

"Seriously?" I asked.

She chuckled at that. "Yes!"

I smiled harder than I've ever smiled before pulling her lips to mine, needing to connect on another level.

"I take it you're happy then."

"Yes! If I can tell everyone, I will. I'll tell the whole fucking world. Thank you, baby. I love you so much," I said, finding her lips again.

"What would you want it to be? I mean a girl or boy?"

"Of course I wouldn't mind a little boy, but then again a little girl that looks just like you would make me happy just as well. It doesn't matter. As long as he or she is healthy. That is the most important thing," I told her.

"I think so too."

As I watched her focus on the game, I realized I couldn't love her more than I already did. Every time I looked at her, something twisted in my chest. It had been that way ever since we had gotten back together. Our love was so strong now, and it warmed my heart that we had finally let go of all the mistakes of our past.

Leah was a beautiful woman, even more so now than before. She loved me. Loved me with all of my flaws. I loved her. It was something so fierce that it shook me to my core. Any time I held her, kissed her, touched her, I knew I was a lucky man. Love had made me absolutely crazy. Crazy for Leah. And I was fine with that. Being addicted to her was worth it because I knew that we would always feel that way about each other. Nothing could ever change that.

The End!

Don't Blame Me

Song Playlist

Backstreet Boys- Show Me the Meaning of Being Lonely

Christina Aguilera- Twice

Ed Sheeran- Perfect

Evanescence- Bring Me to Life

Evanescence- Going Under

Jude Demorest, Ryan Destiny & Brittany O'Grady-

Unlove You

Natalie Imbruglia-Torn

Savage Garden- I Knew I Loved You

Sixpence Non The Richer- Kiss Me

Taylor Swift- Don't Blame Me

The Cardigans- Lovefool

Hawaiian Words Glossary

Aloha au ia'oe- I love you

Hapa haole- person of mixed race

Hāpai- Pregnant

Kai- Sea

Keiki- Child/Children

Kuuipo- Sweetheart

Mahina- Moon

Maika'I no au- I am fine

Mau Loa- Forever

Nani- Pretty

Ohana- Family

Pehea 'oe? - How are you?

About the Author:

Kay is an award winning author of contemporary and interracial romance. Her stories are sweet, sassy and has a touch of sexy in them. She is from arguably the greatest city in the world. (New York). She is a sarcastic sweetheart who prefers snuggling at home with a good book. Kay is a mom of 3 cubs and a wife. Kay indulges in strawberry cheesecake, horror movies, Harry Potter, The Walking Dead, wrestling and of course a happily ever after. She is the creator of Bookish Brown Girls, a platform dedicated to uplifting and supporting books written by women of color.

Follow her:

(Twitter/Instagram/Wattpad/Pinterest)

@authorkayblake

Made in the USA
Middletown, DE
28 July 2023

35840907R00205